The Highlig

Big Book of Science Secrets

101 Amazing Experiments

Parents:

We have prudently prepared the experiments and the activities in this book so that they can be safely performed by children eight years or older. Because children develop at different levels, no one other than a parent can judge the abilities of a particular child. Please review the enclosed experiments to be sure that you are comfortable that they are appropriate for your child.

The Editors
Highlights for Children, Inc.

Boyds Mills Press

Table of Contents

Science Consultants: Jack Myers, Ph.D., Clifford Swartz, Ph.D., Robert A. McHugh

Illustrators: David Celsi, Melissa Crane, Lisa Cypher, Doris Ettlinger, Peter Fasolino, Durell Godfrey, Barbara Gray, Susan Gray, Dennis Hockerman, Joan Holub, Laura Houston, Loretta Lustig, Brenda Pepper, Clare Sieffert, Jerry Zimmerman

Writers: Lisa Feder-Feitel, Laura Jeffers, Renee Skelton, Ingrid Wickelgren, Christina Wilsdon

Publisher Cataloging-in-Publication Data
The Highlights big book of science secrets : puzzles, projects, experiments, and challenges galore / from the editors of Highlights for Children.—1st ed.
[144]p. : col. ill. ; cm.
Includes index.
Summary : Engaging science experiments, puzzles, and projects relating to a broad range of topics including food, weather, water, senses, and light. Organized in steps with clear illustrations.
ISBN 1-56397-651-X
1. Science—Juvenile literature. [1. Science.] I. Title.
500—dc20 1997 CIP
Library of Congress Catalog Card Number 96-86537

Published by Bell Books
Boyds Mills Press, Inc.
A Highlights Company
815 Church Street
Honesdale, Pennsylvania 18431
Printed in the United States of America

First edition, 1997

10 9 8 7 6 5 4 3 2 1

Science Magic

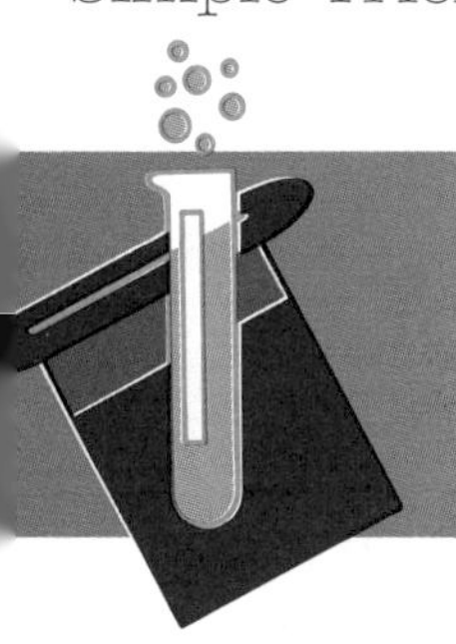

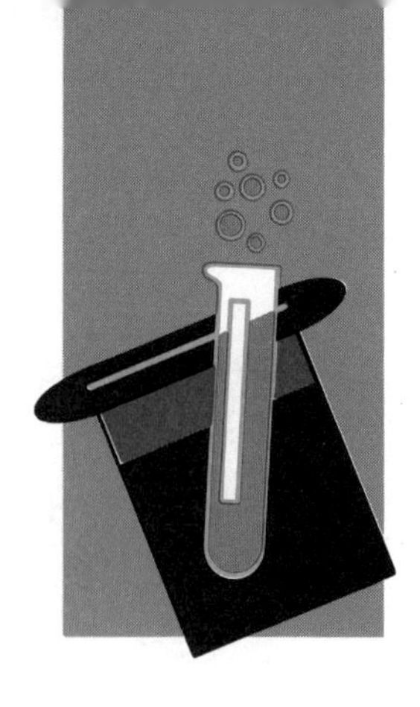

ICE MUSCLES

Do you think water is strong enough to break a pencil? Neither will your friends—until you show them this trick. To perform it, you need three pencils, the toughest tape you can find (like duct tape), and a metal container with a press-on lid. Ask your mom or dad if you can use a small paint can or a car wax can. Make sure you wash the can sparkling clean before you use it.

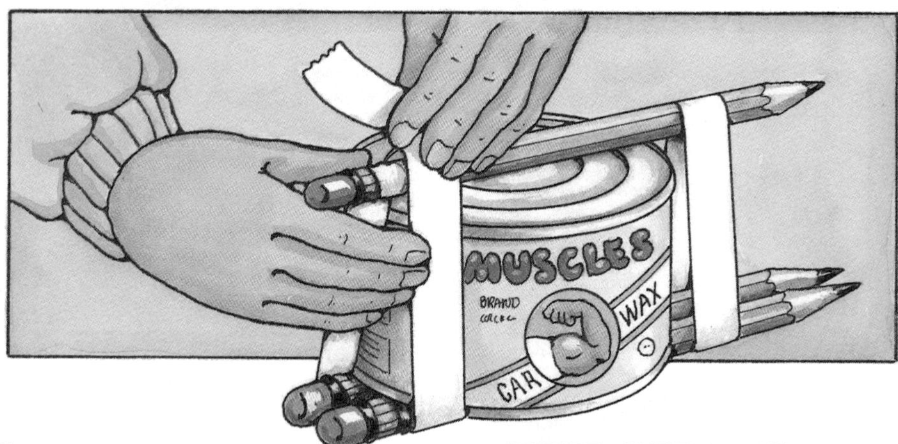

THE TRICK

Fill the container to the very top with water and put the lid on. Tape one pencil over the lid and two pencils to the bottom. Wrap the tape around the pencils as shown in the picture. Make sure the pencils are taped tightly. Place the container in the freezer overnight. The next morning you'll discover that the water has frozen, pushed up the container lid, and broken the top pencil.

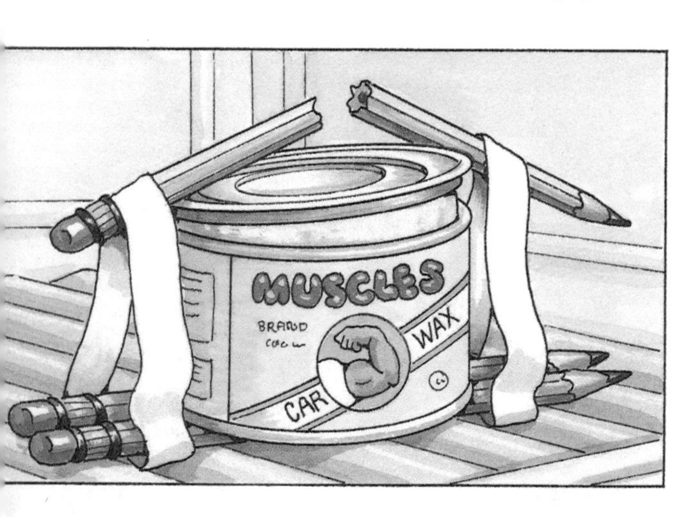

THE SCIENCE SECRET

Most things become smaller when they freeze, but water is different. When water freezes, it expands to take up more space. The pressure of the water turning to ice pushes open the container lid, and the force is strong enough to break the pencil.

This is why the plumbing in houses can become damaged if pipes freeze in winter. The water in the pipes expands and cracks the metal or plastic.

THE VANISHING STAMP

Water is clear, so you expect to be able to see through it. In this trick, a jar of clear water can make a postage stamp disappear. To perform this illusion, you need water, a stamp, and a glass jar with a lid. The jar should have smooth sides. (Many peanut butter or mayonnaise jars work well.)

THE TRICK

Place the stamp faceup on a table. Set the empty jar on top of the stamp and put the lid on. As you move around the table, you can see the stamp through the glass.

Now, keep the jar on top of the stamp. Fill the jar to the top with water and put the lid on. Walk around the table. With the jar filled with water, the stamp remains invisible from every angle.

QUICK TIP

The key to this trick is to find the right jar. It must be smooth on all sides. If the bottom of a jar is curved, the trick might not work. The curved glass may act like a lens so that the stamp can be seen through the water. Try this trick with several jars. After you decide which one works best, you will be ready to perform the trick.

THE SCIENCE SECRET

You are able to see things because light is reflected off whatever you look at.

Light travels at different speeds through different substances. It moves a bit slower through glass and water than it does through air. This causes the rays of light to change direction when they pass from the water and glass into the air. In this case, the rays would have to change direction so much that they cannot even get out of the jar. They reflect right back into the water and never reach your eyes.

FINGER POWER

It's easy to stop a leak in a container with a hole in it—just put your finger over the hole. But do you think you can stop *four* leaks with one finger?

THE TRICK

Find a container with a tight-fitting lid. A plastic container from yogurt, whipped cream, or butter is good to use. With a pencil or scissors, carefully poke four holes in the bottom of the container. Make a single hole in the center of the lid.

Hold the container over the sink or any empty bowl. Fill the container with water, and put on the lid. As you'd expect, water flows through the holes in the bottom.

Fill the container with water again. Before too much leaks out, put your finger on the top hole. The flow stops. Let go, and the water shoots out the bottom holes again. By lifting your finger on and off the top hole, you can control the water's flow.

THE SCIENCE SECRET

When you put your finger on the top hole, you prevent air from going inside. The air pressure underneath the container is then strong enough to keep the water from flowing through the holes in the bottom. When you release your finger, air goes into the container. The air pressure on the top and bottom of the water is now the same, and the water flows out.

AIR POWER

Show your friends a ruler sticking out from under a few sheets of newspaper, and challenge them to lift the sheets by slapping the ruler. It sounds easy, but it's not.

THE TRICK

Lay the sheets of newspaper on a flat tabletop. Then put the ruler under the sheets as shown in the picture. Leave a little less than half the ruler sticking out over the edge of the table.

Now ask your friends to lift up the paper by smacking down on the ruler with their open hand. (Caution your friends to slap the ruler hard, but not too hard—or the ruler might snap in half.)

THE SCIENCE SECRET

In order to lift the paper you need to move a lot of air out of the way. Doing that quickly takes a lot of force.

Now try to do it slowly. You can do it with just one finger. When you press down slowly on the ruler air has time to move in under the newspapers.

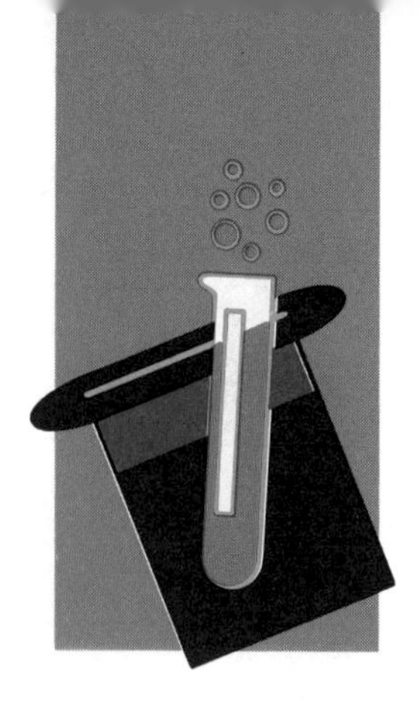

THE ENCHANTED GLASS

Here's a chance to amaze your friends by casting a spell over a glass of water. First, with a few magic words, you will show how an ordinary handkerchief can hold back water in an upside-down glass. Then, while you've really got your audience's attention, you'll describe how—by the sheer power of your concentration—you can cause the water in the glass to bubble.

To do this trick you will need a glass, a rubber band, and a cotton handkerchief.

THE TRICK

Fill a glass almost to the top with water. With your rubber band, attach the cotton handkerchief over the top of the glass, as you see in the picture. Make sure the handkerchief fits tightly over the mouth of the glass.

Say a few magic words, and quickly turn the glass over. The water will stay in the glass as if you've cast a spell over it.

Now, describe how you're going to focus all your mental powers and cause the water to bubble. Secretly slip your index finger under the overturned glass. Each time you press on the center of the handkerchief, bubbles will rise through the glass.

THE SCIENCE SECRET

It seems impossible, but water does not pour out when you turn the glass over. Instead, the water forms a film across the tiny holes in the handkerchief. This film is tight enough to hold back the water in the upside-down glass. When you press with your finger, you break the surface film. Water dribbles out, and air enters the glass and forms the bubbles.

SPLITTING SUNLIGHT

Sunlight is made up of all the colors of the rainbow. But these different colors usually don't show themselves. You can coax them out of hiding with a mirror and a pan of water.

THE TRICK

Fill a flat, square baking pan halfway with water. Place the pan in a spot where sun can shine into it through a window. Put a small mirror into the pan. Prop it up against one side of the pan so the sun's rays shine directly into the mirror. Look on the nearby wall. You should see a rainbow of color.

THE SCIENCE SECRET

The path of a light ray bends when it goes from air into water. Each color within the light bends at a slightly different angle. This spreads out all the colors in a band called a spectrum. The mirror reflects the spectrum back to the wall. And that's where you see the rainbow of colors.

QUICK TIP

You may have to move the pan around a little and to tilt the mirror at various angles. It works best in early morning or late afternoon when the sun is at a low angle. Be patient and keep trying.

TOO HOT OR TOO COLD?

Can a bowl of water feel hot and cold at the same time? Let your fingers find out in this quick trick. All you need are three bowls and some hot water, warm water, and cold water.

THE TRICK

Pour cold water into the first bowl, warm water into the second bowl, and hot water into the third. Place the bowls on a table in front of you.

Dip your left hand into the cold water and your right hand into the hot water. Leave your hands in the water for a full minute. Now, put both hands into the bowl of warm water. Wait—it's not warm anymore, is it? It feels hot—and cold!

THE SCIENCE SECRET

Your skin has nerve endings that sense hot and cold. They work well, but you can fool them. When you dip your hands in the two bowls, one hand feels cold and the other feels hot. When you dip your hands in the warm bowl, the nerves in your fingertips must adjust to the new temperature. Since each hand compares the warm water with the bowl it was just in, the water feels hot and cold at the same time!

QUICK TIP

If you can't feel the difference, try making the cold water colder with ice cubes. The hot water must not be so hot that it will burn your hand.

THE FLOATING CAP

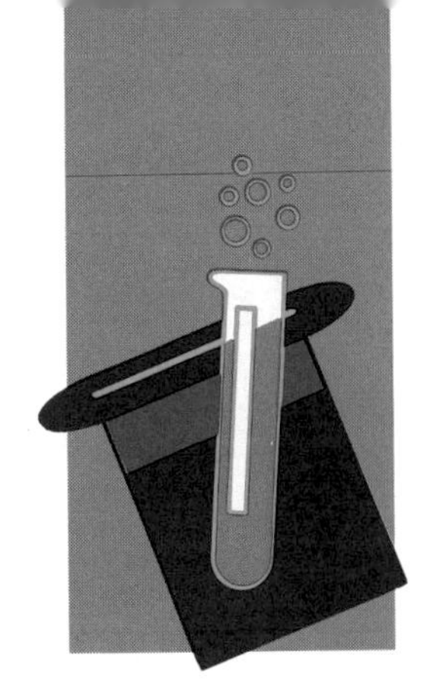

It sounds easy to float a bottle cap. Just hold it upside down, and drop it in a glass of water. But can you make it float in the exact center of the glass? That's not as easy as you think . . . unless you know the secret. To do this trick, you need two glasses of water and a bottle cap.

THE TRICK

Fill the glass almost to the top with water. Hand your friend a bottle cap and challenge her to make it float in the center. No matter how gently she places it in the glass, it drifts to the side.

Now it's your turn. Put some water in a second glass. Slowly pour the water from this glass into the glass with the cap. Make it as full as possible. As the glass fills to the brim, the cap drifts to the center and stays there.

THE SCIENCE SECRET

In the glass that is not full the water curves upward at the edge and wets the glass. The water surface also curves upward around the bottle cap. The surface tension of water pulls these two wet surfaces together. So the bottle cap always floats to the side of the glass.

When you fill the glass superfull of water the surface actually bulges upward. Look carefully and you will see that most of the bulge is close to the glass. Now the surface tension of water forces the bottle cap toward the surface where it has the least amount of upward bulge.

LISTEN WITH YOUR TEETH

Everyone knows ears are made for hearing—but did you ever think you could hear with your teeth? With nothing more than a metal fork and a metal spoon, you can find out.

THE TRICK

With your thumb and index finger, hold the fork in the middle. Bang the spoon against the fork. You will hear a sound, of course. But as the sound begins to fade, put the handle of the fork between your front teeth and bite on it. You'll hear the sound again, through your teeth!

THE SCIENCE SECRET

At first, you hear the sound with your ears because the air carries the sound vibrations from the fork to your ears. But solid things, like teeth, carry sound better than air. Your teeth pick up the vibrations that are still in the fork but are too faint for your ears to hear.

THE SINKING BASKET

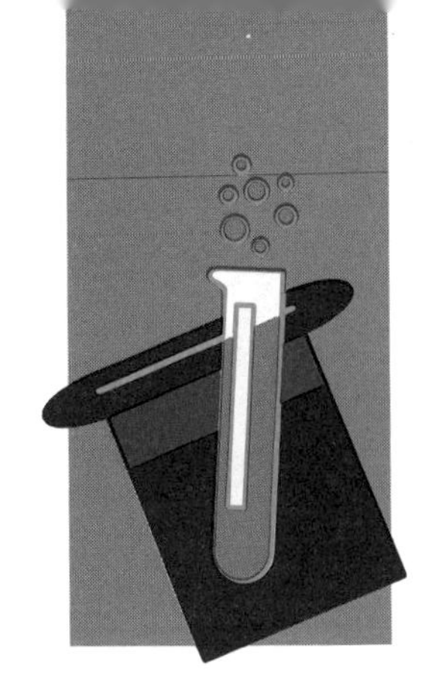

Which weighs more—a quarter or a tissue? Your friends will guess the quarter, until you confuse them with a little magic.

To perform this trick, you need a quarter, tissues, a bowl, and a plastic fruit basket like the one you see in the picture. Strawberries, blueberries, and cherry tomatoes are often packed in baskets like this.

THE TRICK

Fill the bowl with water. Gently place the basket so it floats on the water.

Hand your friend a quarter and a piece of tissue paper. Ask him which weighs more. After holding them in each hand, he will certainly choose the quarter.

Take the quarter and gently place it in the basket. It should float. Now remove the quarter. Carefully place the tissue in the basket. After a few seconds, it sinks!

THE SCIENCE SECRET

It may seem odd that a basket full of holes floats, but an invisible skin on the surface of the water blocks each hole. That prevents the water from flowing into the basket. This skin is strong enough so that the added weight of the quarter does not change a thing.

When you place the tissue in the basket, it soaks up the water through the holes and breaks the invisible skin. Once the skin is broken, water pours in and sinks the basket.

QUICK TIP

It takes a little time for the water to soak into the tissue. While you wait, say a few magic words over the bowl. This gives the water time to break the skin, and makes it seem as if you are casting a magical spell.

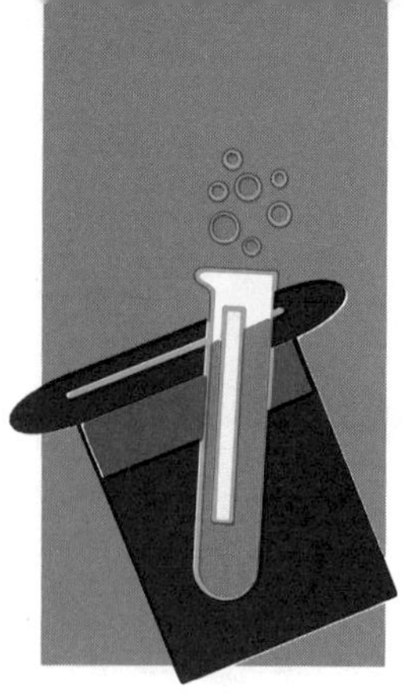

HUFF AND PUFF

Ask your friends if they can blow over a pile of books with their breath. It sounds impossible, but with a plastic bag, books, and some lung power, you can show them how to do it.

THE TRICK

Hand a stack of books to your friends and ask them to blow them over. They'll huff and puff until they're exhausted. When they're convinced it's impossible, you show them the trick.

Put the plastic bag on a tabletop and place the books on the bag. Leave enough of the top of the bag exposed so you can form an opening to blow into. Then start blowing into the bag as if you were blowing up a balloon.

Despite the weight of the books, the bag fills with air. Soon the books will rise and topple over.

THE SCIENCE SECRET

A small difference of pressure on a large area can produce a large total force. When you blow into the bag, you are raising the pressure of the air inside which is pressing outward over the whole area of the bag. The force shoving up on the books is equal to the product of the area under the books and the extra pressure. That force will be enough to raise the books.

THE PUZZLING PLATE

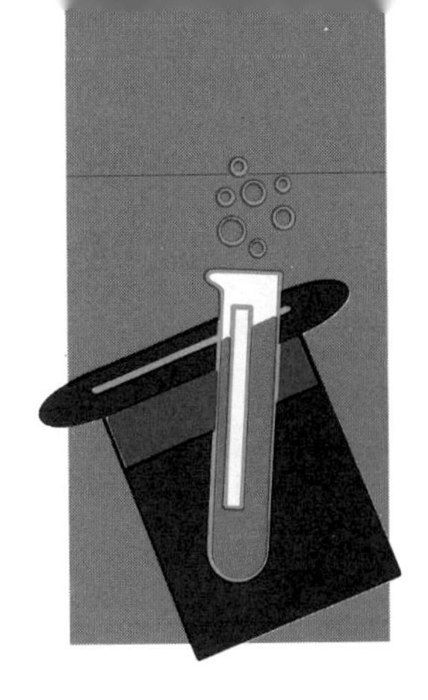

You can create a shape that appears to change size as you move it. You won't believe your eyes . . . and you shouldn't, because your eyes will be playing tricks on you! To perform this magic, you need a paper plate and a pair of scissors.

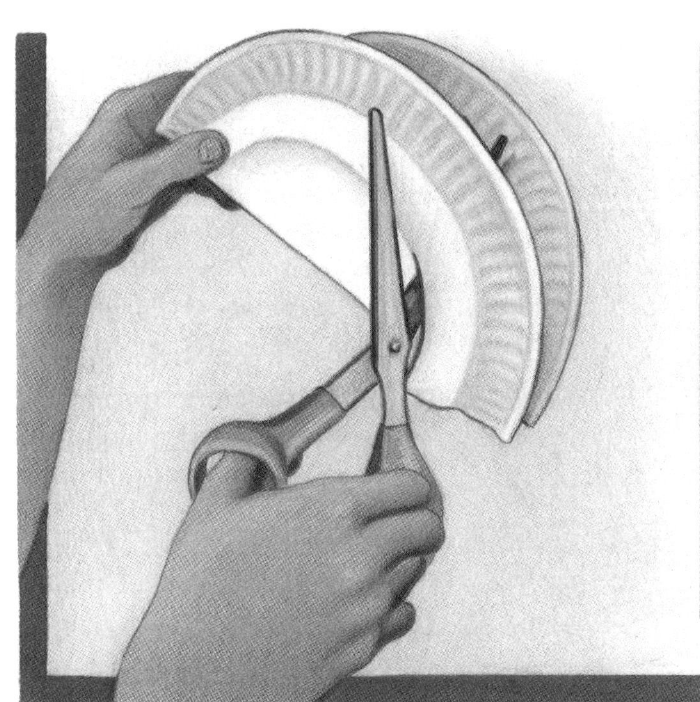

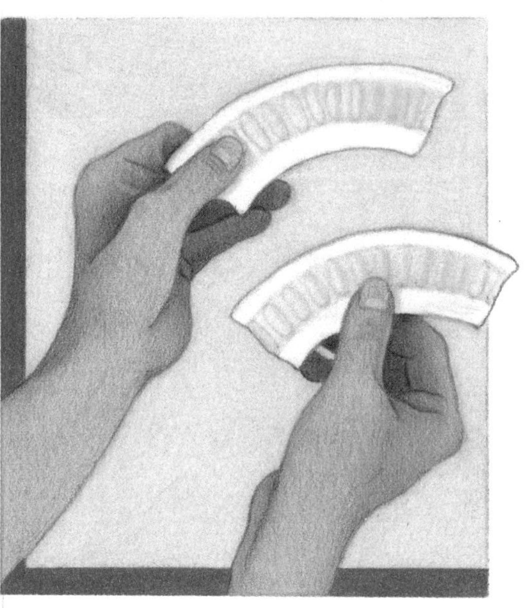

THE TRICK

Fold the paper plate in half and carefully cut it along the crease. Take one half of the plate and snip off its rim. Fold this rim exactly in half, lining up the two ends, and cut along the crease. Now you should have two identical pieces. Place one on top of the other; they should match up exactly.

Slowly move one piece up so it is just above the other piece. Be sure to keep the pieces lined up along one edge. Do the pieces still appear to be the same size? The one above seems smaller. Switch the pieces and see which one is smaller now.

THE SCIENCE SECRET

You know the pieces are the same size, but the top one always seems smaller. Your eyes are playing tricks on you. Instead of comparing the sizes of the two entire pieces, your eyes compare the two curved edges that are closest together. Since you've put the shorter curved edge of one piece next to the longer curved edge of the other, the piece with its shorter edge near its twin looks smaller.

THE HOVERING CARD

When you perform this trick, a glass of water seems to defy the laws of gravity. To work your magic, you need a drinking glass and an index card large enough to cover the opening of the glass.

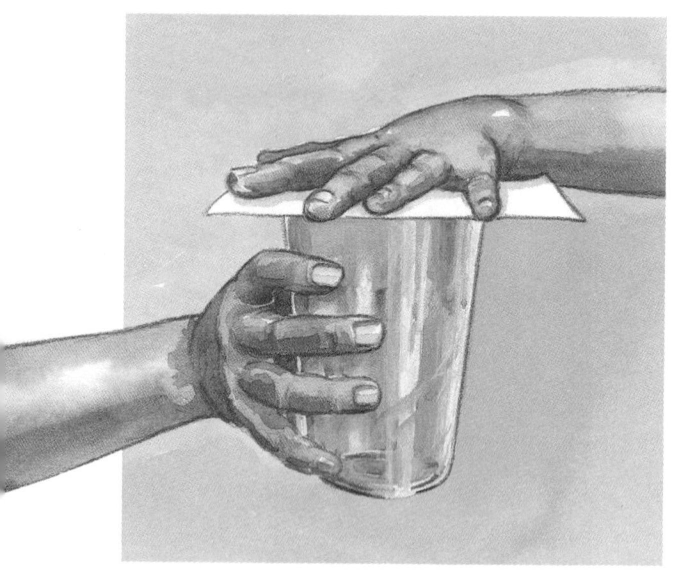

THE TRICK

Fill the glass to the very top with water. Make sure the rim is wet. Slip the index card over the top of the glass. Now hold the card in place and turn the glass over. Wait a moment, and then remove your hand from the bottom. Amazing!

THE SCIENCE SECRET

Right now, you are standing at the bottom of an ocean of air. You don't notice it, but air pressure is all around you.

When you turn the glass over, the water pushes down on the card. The air around you pushes back so the card does not move. Eventually, the card gets soggy, some water seeps out, and air goes into the glass. The balance of forces changes and water comes splashing out.

MIND READING MIRROR

You can't really read your friend's mind. But you'll have her believing you can—when the number she's thinking of suddenly appears on a mirror. All it takes is soap, water, a mirror, and a cotton swab.

THE TRICK

First, fill a pot with soapy water. Dip in a cotton swab. Then use it to write the number 5 on a small hand mirror. Make sure the writing is invisible.

Now tell your friend you can read her mind. To prove it, ask her to pick a number. (She might want to write it down.) Have her double the number she has picked. Then tell her to add 10 and divide by 2. Last of all, tell her to subtract her original number.

Now pretend you are concentrating very hard. Hand your friend the mirror and ask her to breathe on it up close. The number 5 will magically appear. And that will be her number!

THE SCIENCE SECRET

If your friend did the math right, you can't be wrong. The answer is always 5.

When warm, moist air from her breath hits the cooler surface of the mirror, drops of water appear. Her breath covers the mirror with a thin, foggy mist. But an invisible, soapy film remains where you wrote the number 5. This film keeps the fog from sticking there, so the number magically appears.

Did you ever notice how the bathroom mirror fogs up after a shower? Write a soapy message on the mirror for your mom or dad. There will be a big surprise when he or she steps out of the shower.

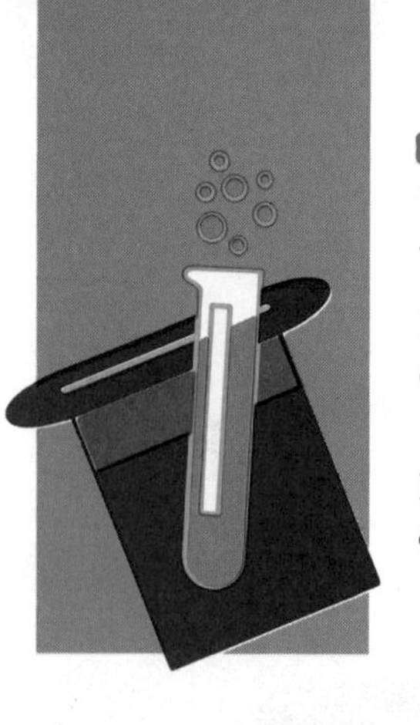

THE REVERSING ARROW

When light passes through water it can produce some surprising results. In this case, it can turn an arrow around.

For this trick you need an index card, a pencil, a round smooth drinking glass, and a pitcher of water.

Draw an arrow on an index card and lean it against a wall. Now, tell your audience that you can make the arrow point in the other direction *without touching the card.*

Place the empty glass in front of the card. Slowly fill it with water. As the glass fills, the arrow turns and faces the other direction!

QUICK TIP

When you first try this trick, slide the glass of water forward and back in front of the card. The distance between the glass and the index card determines how well the trick works. Figure out the best distance before you perform the trick.

THE SCIENCE SECRET

When you look at the arrow through the empty glass, it looks pretty normal. The glass bends the light a bit, but not enough to change what you see.

As you pour the water, it takes on the curved shape of the glass. This creates a thick lens through which the light must travel on its way to your eyes. The water lens bends the rays of light. This causes the image to reverse and the arrow to look as if it's pointing the other way.

BURP IN A BOTTLE

It takes a lot of breath to blow up a balloon, but you can do it without any huffing and puffing. You'll need a balloon, vinegar, baking soda, a tissue, water, and a narrow-necked bottle, like the kind used for catsup or soy sauce.

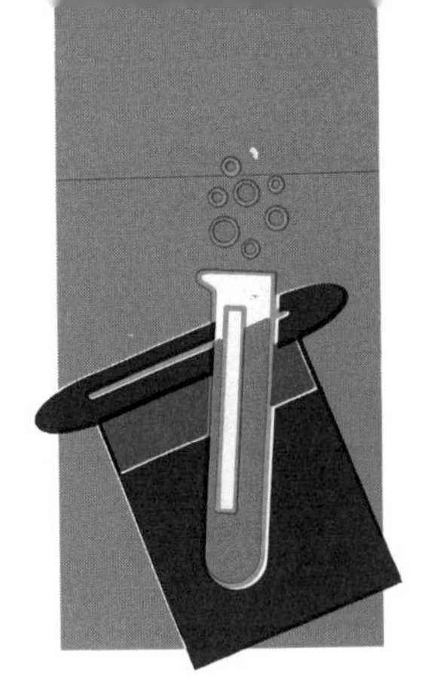

THE TRICK

Fill the bottle a quarter of the way with vinegar. Fill most of the rest of the bottle with water. Leave about one inch of air at the top.

Wrap a teaspoon of baking soda tightly in a small piece of tissue paper. Make the baking soda packet small enough to fit into the bottle's opening.

Slide the packet into the bottle and quickly place the balloon over the bottle top. The liquid inside will start to fizz and foam. Then watch the balloon fill up with air.

THE SCIENCE SECRET

The mixing of vinegar and baking soda causes the fizzing inside the bottle. It also gives off a gas—carbon dioxide. This gas rises through the bottle and into the balloon and blows it up.

TRY THIS

Take the balloon off the bottle. Pinch it tight to trap the gas inside. Then, put it into your mouth and let out some of the gas. Don't worry—it's harmless. Does it remind you of the taste when you burp after a long drink of cold soda? Carbon dioxide gas is used to give soda pop its fizz.

WATER WEAVING

Do you think you can weave water? With this trick, you'll discover a very curious thing about water—it's so sticky, you can tie it in knots.

THE TRICK

Take an empty plastic soda bottle. With the tip of a pencil, poke three holes near the bottom of the bottle. Try to get the holes in a straight line about a quarter of an inch apart. Then, fill the bottle with water. As you might expect, the water shoots out the three holes.

Now, rub your thumb and forefinger over the holes. See if you can weave those three streams into one big stream. It might take a few tries to get it right, but soon you'll be tying water in knots like an expert.

THE SCIENCE SECRET

Tiny particles of water tend to stick together. By pinching the streams with your fingers, you've made the water stick together to form one big stream. You can separate the streams again by moving your finger over each of the holes.

THE DISAPPEARING GLASS

You can make a glass disappear right before your friend's eyes. All you need is a large glass jar with a wide mouth, a small drinking glass, and some cooking oil.

THE TRICK

Place the glass inside the jar. Then tell a friend that by simply saying a few magic words you will make the glass vanish.

While saying your magic words, pour the cooking oil into the glass. Keep pouring as the oil spills over the glass into the jar. Be careful that it doesn't spill out of the jar. As the oil fills the jar, the glass will disappear.

STUMPER

Carefully pour the oil back into its container. Wash out the jar. Repeat the trick using water instead of oil. How does the drinking glass appear?

THE SCIENCE SECRET

When you first set up this magic trick, it's easy to see the glass inside your jar. As light passes from the air through the glass, it changes speed and bends a little bit. But this slight change in direction still allows you to see the glass.

When you add oil to the jar, things change. Light travels at the same speed through oil and glass, so it does not bend. And without that slight change in direction you can no longer see the clear glass.

THE BURSTING BALLOON

Here's a hot trick for a cold winter day. Tell a friend you can make a perfectly good balloon burst without going near it. Your prediction will come true—if you leave the balloon in the right place.

THE TRICK

Blow up a balloon as much as you can without bursting it. Place the balloon near a radiator. Use a piece of tape to keep it there. After a while you will forget about it until suddenly you hear it pop.

THE SCIENCE SECRET

When air becomes warmer, it expands to take up more space. The air inside the balloon expanded because you put it in a very warm spot. The warm air expanded so much that it finally burst the balloon.

QUICK TIP

Make sure you blow the balloon up as much as possible. If you leave room for more air in the balloon, it will expand without bursting.

SWIMMING POPCORN

You can make popcorn swim in a glass of bubbling water. To perform this trick, you need a dozen kernels of unpopped popcorn, vinegar, and baking soda.

THE TRICK

Put a heaping tablespoon of baking soda into a tall drinking glass. In a smaller glass, put a tablespoon of vinegar, and fill this glass with water. Now hold the tall glass over the sink and pour the vinegar water into it. You will see lots of fizzing and bubbling.

Add the popcorn kernels to the glass. At first, the kernels sink to the bottom. Then some of them float to the top of the glass, only to sink again. Up and down they go. As you watch, your popcorn will "swim" up and down for several minutes.

THE SCIENCE SECRET

When you mix baking soda and vinegar, they produce carbon dioxide gas. You can see these gas bubbles in the glass. Some bubbles attach to each popcorn kernel. When enough of these attach, the kernel rises toward the top of the glass. When it reaches the top, the bubbles escape into the air, and the kernel sinks again.

TRY THIS

Repeat this magic trick using raisins, small pieces of spaghetti, or coffee grounds. Can you think of any other things that might swim? Why do you think some things work better than others?

THE SPINNING SNAKE

You can make a snake dance as if by magic. Only you will know the secret.

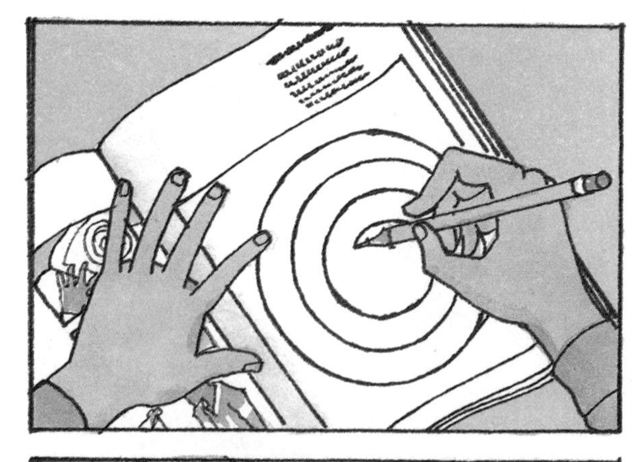

THE TRICK

Trace the spiral on the opposite page. Copy it onto heavy construction paper. Color it to look like a snake. Pull a string through the center of the snake's head and knot the end.

Tell your friends you know a song that will make the snake dance. Hold the snake above a radiator that's giving off heat. Hum a tune, or sing a song. After a few seconds, the snake will start to spin.

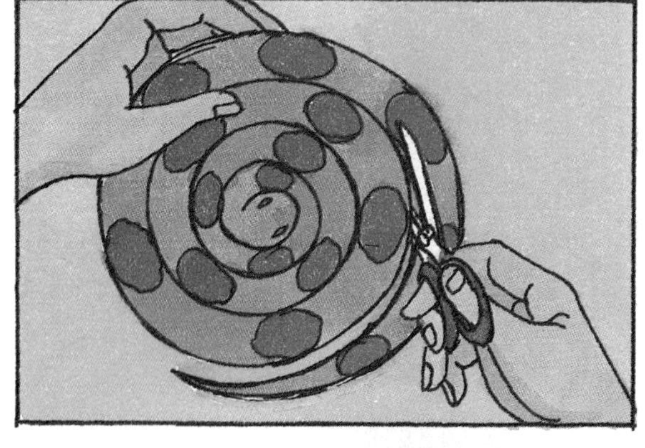

THE SCIENCE SECRET

Moving air makes the snake spin. The radiator heats the air above it. The warm air rises, and cooler air rushes in to take its place. Then *that* air warms and rises, too. This cycle of moving air keeps your snake spinning.

Make a spinning snake mobile. Trace and color several snakes. Using string and a coat hanger, hang them above a radiator. Whenever the heat goes on, your snake mobile will spin.

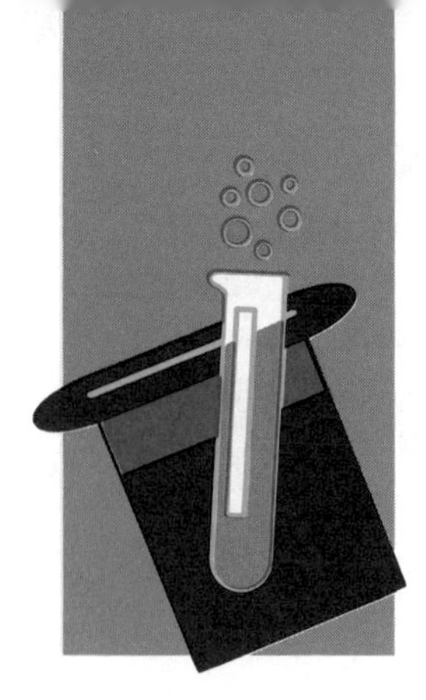

POTION MAGIC

To create a bit of mystery for your friends, you can change the color of grape juice to black. Then, with a few magic words and a secret solution, you can make your potion fizz, and the grape juice will return to its original color. To do this trick, you need baking soda, white vinegar, water, a few glasses, and some purple grape juice.

THE TRICK

Mix equal parts of water and grape juice to fill your first glass halfway. In a second glass half filled with water, stir one tablespoon of baking soda. Mix a tablespoon of vinegar into a third glass that is half filled with water.

Slowly stir a tablespoon of baking soda solution from your second glass into the first glass. The grape juice will turn black. Now, say some magic words and pour some of the vinegar solution from the third glass into the first glass. Presto, the solution will fizz up, and the grape juice returns to its original color.

THE SCIENCE SECRET

Grape juice contains acid and has a purple color. But baking soda is a base, the opposite of an acid. When you add baking soda to the juice, it turns black. Vinegar is also an acid. When you add it to your mixture, it reverses the chemical balance. The extra acid turns the grape juice back to its original color.

THE JINGLING COIN

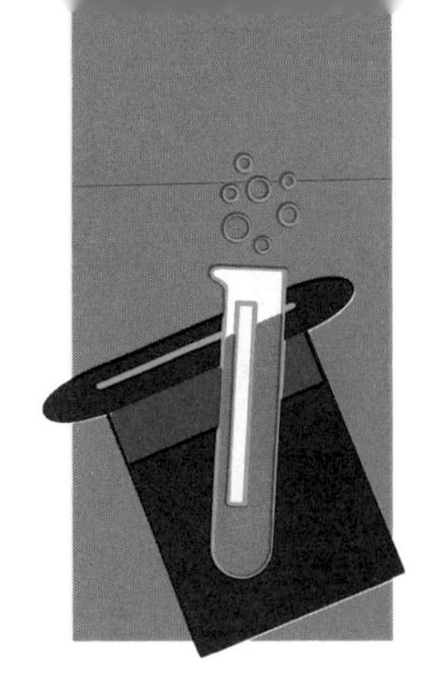

As air gets warmer, it expands and rises. You can't see this when it happens, but you can use this science fact to perform a simple magic trick. You will need a glass bottle with a narrow neck, a coin, and a bowl of hot water. The coin should fit snugly on top of the bottle. (A one-quart glass vinegar bottle and a penny work well together.)

THE TRICK

Place the empty bottle in the freezer for one or two hours, until the bottle is icy cold. (It will probably be covered with a fine layer of frost.)

When the bottle is ready, take the bowl and fill it halfway with hot water. Set it on a table.

Remove the bottle from the freezer. Moisten the top and place the coin over the opening. For this trick to work, the coin must make a seal at the mouth of the bottle.

Stand the bottle in the bowl of hot water. In a few seconds the coin will pop up a little and then fall back with a clink. It will slowly repeat this: clink, clink, clink.

THE SCIENCE SECRET

The heat from the water warms the cold air inside the bottle. As it warms, the air expands. If the coin seals the mouth of the bottle, the air inside cannot get out, and air pressure increases. When the pressure inside is great enough, it pushes up the coin and lets out a spurt of air. Then the coin falls back with a clinking sound.

THE MAGIC TOUCH

Pick a penny, any penny . . . and it will be the one that your friends just chose. How can you do it? The secret is in your fingertips.

THE TRICK

Have five pennies ready, each with a different date. Make sure the pennies are cool to the touch. Place them in front of you and ask a friend to choose one while your back is turned. Ask your friend to hold it tightly, to let his "vibrations" flow into it. Then tell your friend to note the date on the penny in order to remember which one he chose.

After about 20 seconds, have your friend pass the penny to a second friend to hold. Ask her to squeeze the penny tightly and to concentrate on the coin's date. When she's finished, have her put the penny back and then tell you to turn around. You will quickly pick up each penny, and before your friends can say "Abraham Lincoln," you will show them the penny they chose!

THE SCIENCE SECRET

Copper is a good conductor, or carrier, of heat. When your friends squeeze the penny, it absorbs heat from their hands. When you quickly pick up and touch each penny, the nerve endings in your fingers can tell which penny is warmer than the others. That is the penny your friends were holding.

QUICK TIP

To make sure that the pennies are cool to the touch, put them in the refrigerator for a few minutes before you try this trick. Be careful not to let them get too cold, or your friends may guess how you do the trick. And try not to handle them too much once they have cooled off.

THE RUBBER EGG

Ask your friends if they've ever seen an egg laid by a rubber chicken. They'll say there is no such thing, until you bounce an egg in front of them. To do this trick you need water, vinegar, a measuring cup, and a hard-boiled egg.

THE TRICK

The next time Mom or Dad cooks hard-boiled eggs, ask for one for yourself.

Mix a half cup of water with a half cup of vinegar. Put your egg in and leave it for a day. Then carefully take it out and wash it under a faucet. You are now ready to present your rubber egg to your friends. Let them hold it. They can even bounce it a bit. If they don't believe it came from a rubber chicken, ask them how it got the way it is. They'll never guess.

THE SCIENCE SECRET

Eggshells contain calcium, which makes them hard. Acid in your vinegar solution slowly eats away at the calcium in the eggshell. After a day in the solution, the thin remaining shell has been softened by the vinegar so that it becomes rubbery.

QUICK TIP

Make sure the egg stays in the vinegar and water for at least 24 hours. If you don't leave it in long enough, the shell will not get soft and rubbery.

THE CURVING LINES

When is a straight line not straight? When you bend it into a circle! For this trick you need an index card, a ruler, a pencil, and some tape.

THE TRICK

Using your ruler and pencil, draw a series of straight lines on the index card. Poke a hole through the center of the card. Push your pencil through the hole and tape it to the underside of the card.

Place the pencil between your hands and slowly rub them back and forth. As the card spins, the lines start to curve. Move your hands faster, and the lines form perfect circles.

THE SCIENCE SECRET

Your magic trick works because you have created an optical illusion. Sometimes when things are moving, it is difficult for your brain to make sense of what your eyes see. In this case, because the lines are moving in circles, they appear to your eyes as circles.

STUMPER **Is each circle made from a single turning line, or do the lines blend in some other way? Here's an easy way to find out. Repeat this trick, but this time use colored markers instead of a pencil. Draw every line on the card with a different bright color. Now spin your index card. Does each line make its own circle?**

THE MYSTERY PENNY

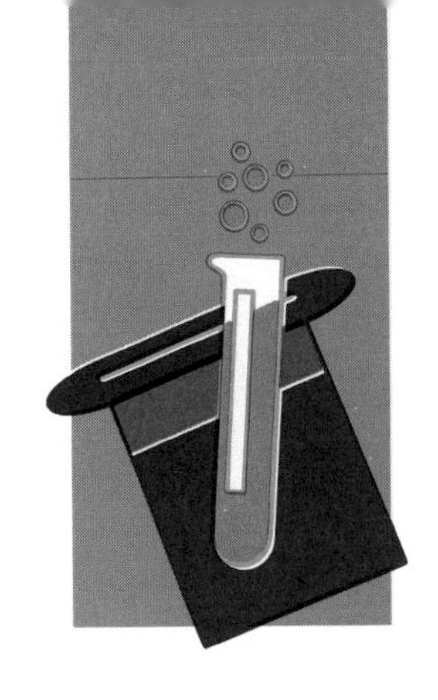

Does money ever slip through your fingers? In this trick, your slipping fingers turn two pennies into three.

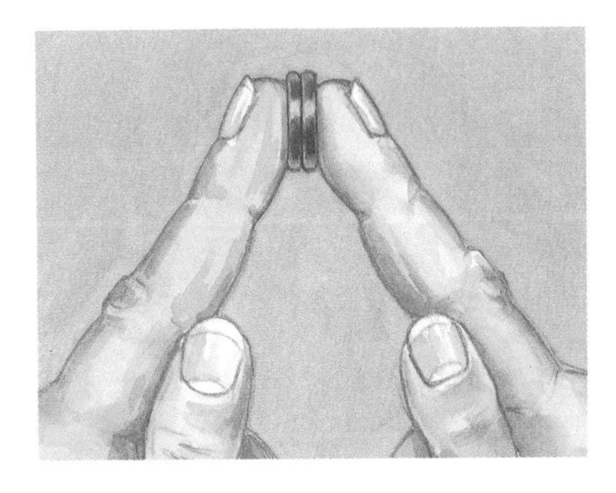

THE TRICK

Place two pennies between your fingers, as you see in the picture. Move your fingers up and down slightly so that the pennies rub against each other. Rub them as fast as you can with short, quick movements. Suddenly, a third penny appears between the other two!

TRY THIS

You can prove that your two eyes see things differently. Hold your finger about six inches in front of your nose, and close one eye. Quickly open that eye and close the other one. Your finger seems to move as you look at it with first one eye and then the other.

THE SCIENCE SECRET

You have just performed a simple optical illusion. It works because you see things with two eyes. Since your eyes are a few inches apart, the picture sent to your brain from each eye is a little different.

Usually your brain puts together the pictures from both eyes. But when you move the pennies quickly, your brain can't quite keep up. It tries to make sense of what it sees. As a result, a mysterious third penny appears.

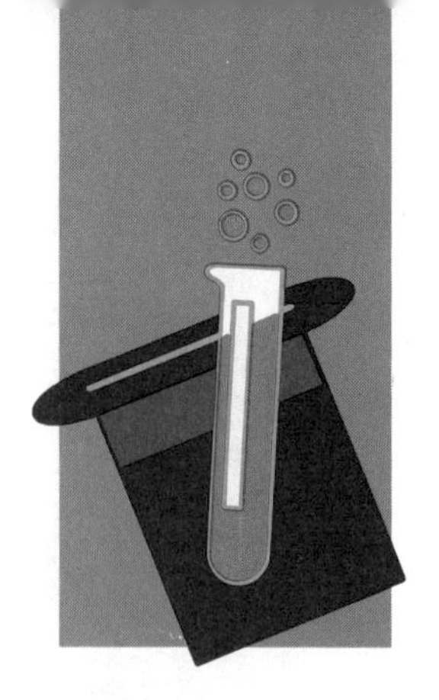

ICE CUBE COWBOY

Can you rope a slippery ice cube? It's easy when you know the trick. All you need is an ice cube, a piece of cotton thread, and a salt shaker.

THE TRICK

Wet the thread and lay one end on the ice cube. Now, sprinkle a good amount of salt over the cube and thread. Wait a few minutes, and then slowly lift.

Take two ice cubes of the same size and place them on a plate. Wrap one in black construction paper and the other in white construction paper. Place the plate in a sunny window. Which ice cube will melt first? Check every 30 minutes to see if you guessed right.

THE SCIENCE SECRET

Salt lowers the temperature at which water freezes. When you sprinkle the cube with salt, the ice begins to melt. As the cube melts, some of the salt washes away. Then the water around the thread freezes again. Now the thread is trapped in the frozen cube. When you lift the thread, the ice cube lifts, too.

HOW MANY MARBLES?

An optical illusion occurs when your eyes play tricks on you. Here's an illusion in which your sense of touch plays tricks on you. To try it, you'll need some marbles and a friend.

THE TRICK

First try this trick on yourself. Cross your first two fingers and touch a marble in between them as you see in the picture. The single marble will feel like two marbles.

Now see if you can fool a friend. Blindfold him, or let him close his eyes. Then have him hold his hand just above a table. Move a few marbles around on the table so your friend can hear them. Then ask him to cross his first two fingers. Hold a single marble between your friend's fingers. Ask him how many marbles he feels. He will probably think he is touching two marbles.

THE SCIENCE SECRET

When your friend's fingers are crossed, the marble touches the *outside* edges of his two fingers. His brain, using common sense, thinks it takes two marbles to touch the outside edges of two fingers.

THE FLOATING COIN

You can use an ordinary glass of water to make a coin mysteriously "appear" in the middle of a bowl.

THE TRICK

Place a coin to one side on the bottom of a round bowl. Have a friend step back from the bowl until the coin is hidden by the bowl's edge. Now tell him that you have some magic water. You will use the water to make the coin move to the center of the bowl.

Tell your friend to watch closely. Then pour the "magic water" slowly into the bowl. The coin will gradually come into view. To your friend, it will seem as if the coin is moving toward the center of the bowl.

QUICK TIP

Make sure you pour the water into the bowl slowly. If you do not, the coin may move and ruin the trick.

THE SCIENCE SECRET

Normally, light travels in a straight line. Your friend can't see the coin at first because the bowl's edge blocks it from view. But the path of the light reflected from the coin bends as it passes from water into air. As the water level rises, the light leaves the surface at a higher and higher point. Finally the rays can pass over the edge of the bowl and enter your friend's eyes.

HOLE IN YOUR HAND

When was the last time you really looked at your hands? This trick lets you look right through them!

THE TRICK

Roll a sheet of paper into a tube. With your right hand, hold the tube up to your right eye, and look through it. Place your left hand against the tube as shown in the picture. Keep both eyes open. You can see right through the hole in your hand!

TRY THIS

Look through the tube with your right eye. Now try sliding your left hand toward and away from you. What happens to the hole?

THE SCIENCE SECRET

Whenever you look at something, each eye sees it from a slightly different angle. Your brain blends these images to give you an accurate picture. But in this trick your eyes see two completely different pictures. One eye sees your hand, and the other sees the hole at the end of the tube. When your brain combines these images, you end up with a hole in your hand.

STICKY STRIPS

Ask a friend what will happen when he blows between two strips of paper. He'll probably say that the strips will move away from each other. Try it and see.

THE TRICK

Cut two strips from a newspaper. Make them about an inch wide and ten inches long. Hold one piece in each hand, between your thumb and index finger. Keep the papers about two inches apart, and have your friend blow between the papers.

Surprise! The papers move toward each other instead of away from each other.

THE SCIENCE SECRET

When your friend blows between the papers, the fast-moving air is at lower pressure than the air outside the strips. Since the air pressure outside is greater, the strips of paper are shoved together.

TRY THIS

Another way to see the same effect is by holding two pieces of 8½ x 11 inch paper in front of you. Put them close together and try to blow between them. Instead of moving apart, they will come together.

Plans and Projects

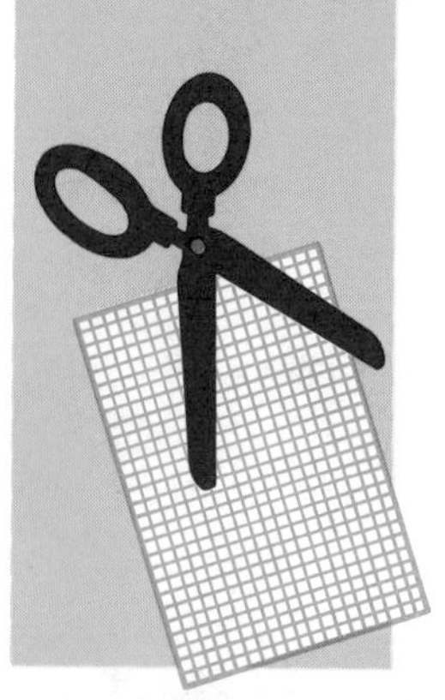

TAKE THE TASTE TEST

What's your favorite food? Ice cream? Pretzels? Grapefruit? Pickles? All tastes you sense can be put into four groups: sweet, salty, bitter, or sour. Do you know how your tongue tells one taste from another? Take the taste test and find out.

MATERIALS

Warm water
Salt
4 paper cups
Apple juice
Unsweetened grapefruit juice
Lemon juice
Paper and pencil
Cotton swabs
Blindfold
A willing friend

WHAT YOU DO

1. Draw a picture of your tongue that looks like the one on this page.

2. Shake a teaspoon of salt into a cup; then add water. Fill a second cup with apple juice, a third cup with grapefruit juice, and a fourth cup with lemon juice. Label the cups, and place a cotton swab in each one.

3. Blindfold your friend, and ask her to stick out her tongue. Take the swab from the salt water, and gently touch it to region 1 of your friend's tongue. Ask her how it tastes. Is it salty, sweet, bitter, or sour?

4. Mark the results on the tongue drawing. Use SA for salty; SW for sweet; B for bitter; SO for sour.

5. Do the taste test on the other regions of the tongue. Then have your friend rinse her mouth with clean water. Repeat the test using the apple juice, grapefruit juice, and lemon juice. Mark the results on your drawing of the tongue.

6. Test all four liquids again. Make sure to use clean cups and swabs for each test. What has the tongue told you?

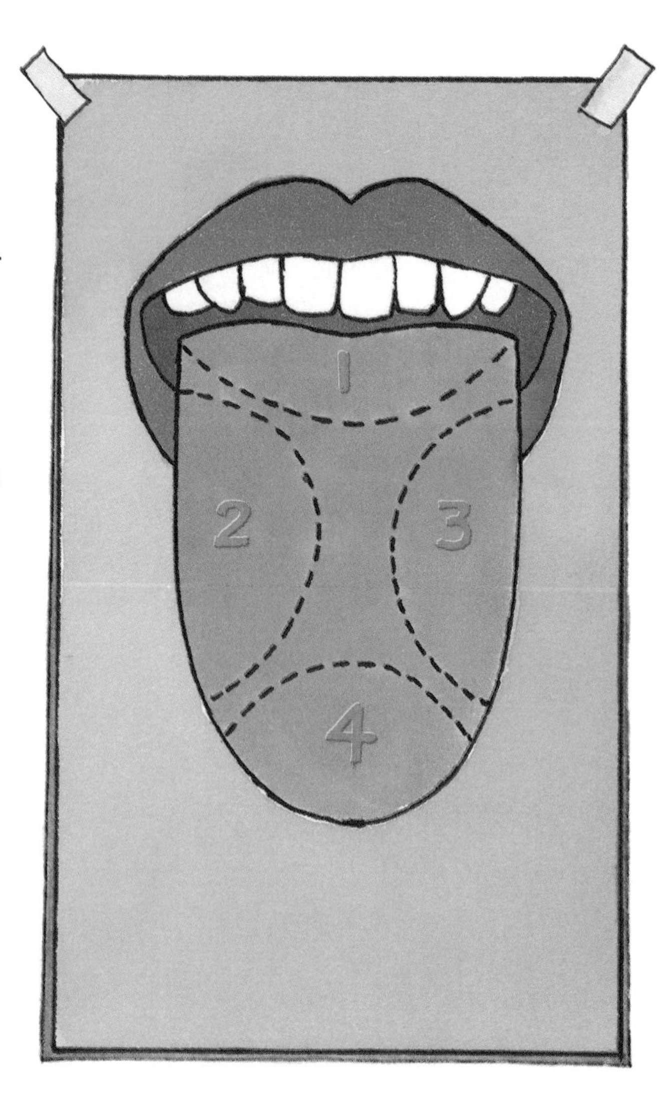

WHY IT WORKS

Look at your tongue in the mirror. The rosy bumps you see are your taste buds. They sense whether things taste salty, sweet, bitter, or sour. Different parts of your tongue sense each of these four types of taste. You taste sweetness at the tip of your tongue, saltiness at the tip and sides, sourness behind the salty areas, and bitterness at the back.

FAT SLEUTH

With a little detective work, you can find out which foods are lean and which are filled with hidden fat.

MATERIALS

Brown paper grocery bag
Pen or pencil
Samples of some of your favorite foods
 You may want to try these pairs:
  Pretzel/Potato chip
  Banana/Avocado
  Peanut butter/Jelly
  Bagel/Donut
  Chunk of chocolate/Piece of hard candy
  Olive/Grape
  Chunk of cheese/Piece of potato

WHAT YOU DO

1. Choose several pairs of foods you'd like to test.

2. Cut a big piece out of the paper bag. Draw one line down the center of the piece of paper and several lines across. You should draw enough horizontal lines to make boxes for all your food samples.

3. Write the name of each food in a box. Keep the foods in each pair side by side.

4. Put the paper on a clean tabletop and dab a bit of each food on the space near its name. Rub any solid food—especially the dry ones—against the paper. (Wash your hands after handling each sample so you don't transfer any of it to the next one.)

5. Remove any excess food stuck to the paper and set the paper to dry. Wait several hours or overnight.

6. Hold the piece of paper up to the light and compare the stains left by the various foods on your chart. The fattiest foods will have the biggest stains. Use this chart to help you make healthier food choices.

WHY IT WORKS

Fat and water ooze out of the foods and trickle between the paper's fibers. They make the paper shiny because they let light through the fibers. As the paper dries, the water evaporates. After a few hours, the stain you see is all fat.

MOVIES IN MOTION

Sometimes you'll hear people say "Seeing is believing." What they mean is that if you see something, you can be sure it is true. But can you? Your eyes play tricks on you all the time. You can "see" for yourself by making some simple eye-foolers.

MATERIALS

Pencils
Thin white paper
Scissors
Paste
Index cards
Tape

WHAT YOU DO

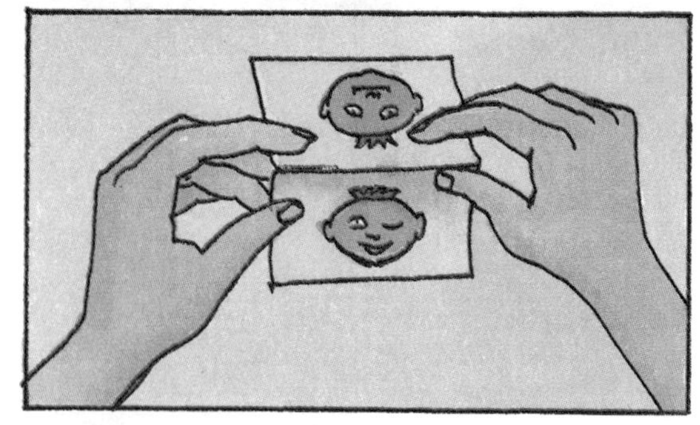

1. Each pair of pictures on the next page will make an eye-fooler. Start with the rectangle with two pictures of a winking man. Trace the rectangle and the pictures onto a thin piece of paper.

2. Cut out the rectangle shape and paste it onto an index card. Make sure that the line down the middle of the rectangle is in the middle of the index card.

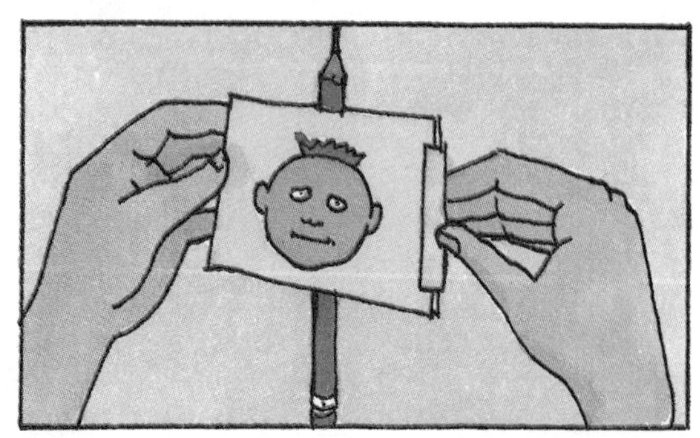

3. Fold the card in half along the center line. Poke a small hole through the fold in the center of the card.

4. Stick a pencil through the hole. Then fold down the sides and tape them in place. Tape the bottom side of the card to the pencil, too.

5. Try out your eye-fooler. Hold the pencil in the palms of your hands. Move your palms back and forth so that the pencil spins. What happens to the two pictures?

6. Repeat steps one through five to make your other eye-foolers.

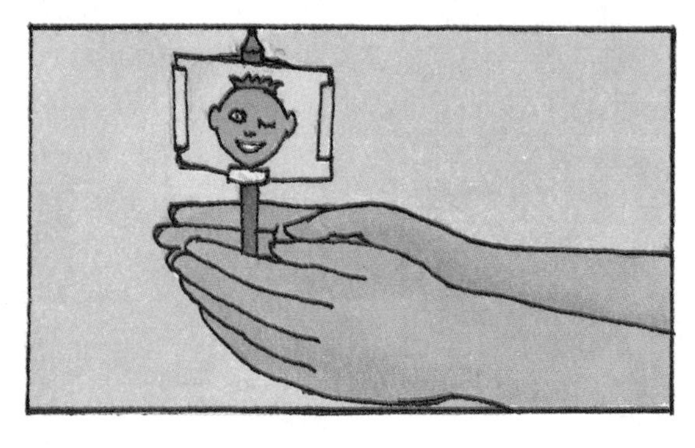

WHY IT WORKS

When your eyes stare at something, a message about what you see goes to your brain. This happens in an instant. As you spin the pencil back and forth, two pictures are sent to the brain. Before the first one disappears, your brain sees the second one. The result is an optical illusion. You see two pictures together.

QUICK TIP

To help see your moving pictures, hold the pencil at arm's length when you spin it. Try spinning it at different speeds to see which works best.

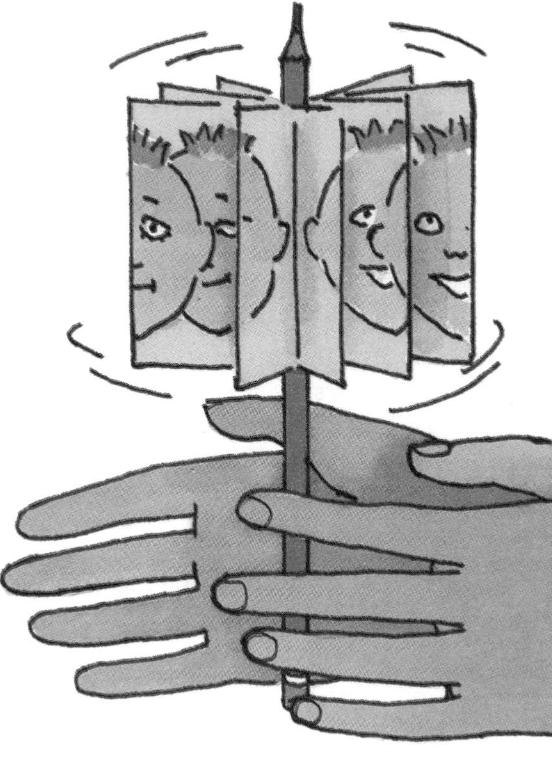

MAKE A WIND SPINNER

Have you ever wondered how fast the wind blows? You can make an instrument to measure the speed of the wind. It's called an anemometer.

MATERIALS

Four paper cups
A red felt-tip marker
Two strips of 1 inch x 18 inch cardboard
Tape or a stapler
Scissors
The cap of a ball-point pen
Wire coat hanger

WHAT YOU DO

1. Cross the cardboard strips in the middle so they form an X. Staple or tape them together.

2. Carefully make a hole in the center of the X with the scissors. Make the hole big enough so that the end of the pen cap will fit into it. Don't make it so big that the pen cap goes straight through it.

3. Use the red felt-tip marker to color one of the paper cups.

4. Cut lengthwise slits in the sides of each paper cup, and fit it onto one of the ends of the cardboard X. Face all the cups in the same direction.

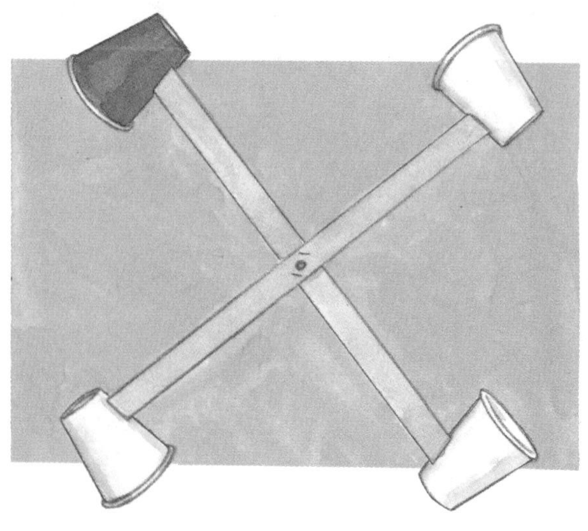

5. Untwist the top of the hanger. Straighten it out and then break it in the middle. (You might want to ask a parent to do this for you.) Use only one half of the hanger. Find a place outdoors where you can stick one end of the hanger deep into the ground. Fit the pen cap into the hole you made in the cardboard X and balance the X on the end of the hanger.

6. To measure the speed of the wind, count how many times the red cup goes around in one minute. Divide this number by ten, and the result is approximately how many miles the wind is traveling per hour.

WHY IT WORKS

When the wind blows, it fills up the cup that is facing into it and pushes that cup away. The anemometer turns, and the next cup moves to face into the wind. Then that cup fills up with wind and gets pushed away. Because there is always one cup facing into the wind, the anemometer keeps turning as long as the wind is blowing.

TRY THIS

Make a wind sock. Cut off one leg of an old pair of pantyhose. Thread a piece of wire through the top of the leg, making a loop. Tie three long pieces of string to the wire at intervals. Push a long stick into the ground and attach the other ends of the strings to the top of the stick. When the wind blows, it will fill up the wind sock and show you which way the wind is blowing.

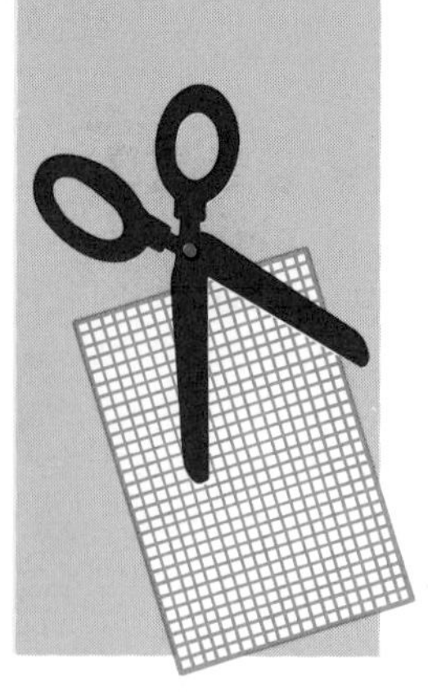

CABBAGE DETECTOR

How do you know a lemon is sour? By tasting it, of course. But there's a way to find out whether a food is sour without tasting it. You can turn half a head of cabbage into a taste-tester.

MATERIALS

Half a head of red cabbage
Two large bowls
A colander or strainer
Several clean glasses or paper cups
Hot water
Lemon juice
Vinegar
A measuring cup
A spoon

WHAT YOU DO

1. Break the cabbage into small pieces. Put them into a large bowl and carefully add 2 cups of hot tap water. Stir and then let stand for 15 to 20 minutes, or until the water turns purple.

2. Use the colander to strain the purple liquid into the second bowl.

3. Fill a glass halfway with the liquid. Add a little bit of lemon juice. What color does the liquid become?

4. Half-fill another glass with the liquid and add some vinegar. The cabbage juice has the same color it did when you added the lemon juice.

WHY IT WORKS

Foods like lemons and vinegar are sour because they contain acids. Your cabbage juice will always turn pink when combined with an acid. For this reason, the cabbage juice is called an indicator. Because it always turns the same color when combined with an acid, it is useful for testing whether foods contain acid.

TRY THIS

Test some other foods, like baking soda and cola. Baking soda is the opposite of an acid. It is called a base. Your mixture will always turn greenish blue when combined with a base. Try out other foods. If the mixture doesn't change color at all, the food you are testing is neutral, neither an acid nor a base.

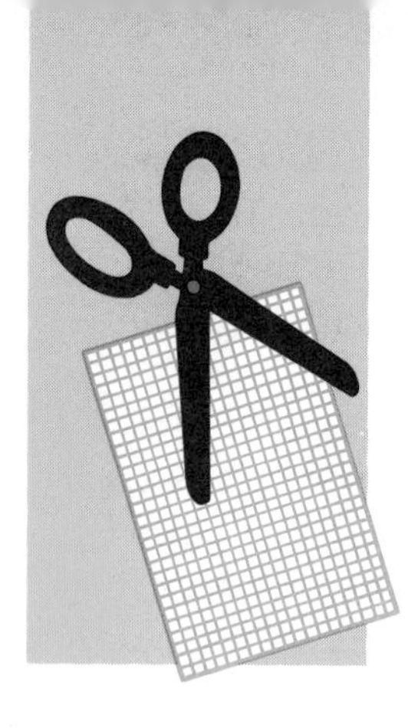

CEREAL BOX CAMERA

You can turn a cereal box into a kind of camera. Point it out the window and you will see a miniature picture show right inside the box.

MATERIALS

An empty cereal box
Scissors
Wax paper
A pin
Tape

WHAT YOU DO

1. Measure your cereal box to make sure it is at least 12 inches tall. Remove the wax paper from the inside and throw it away.

2. You must now make a flap in the box. It should look just like the picture on the right. Take your scissors and cut across the middle of the box. Now cut down one side. Finally cut across the bottom so the flap opens.

3. Take a smooth piece of wax paper that is about two inches high. Tape both sides so the paper is standing two inches from the bottom of the box. Be sure there are no wrinkles or creases in your wax paper. The smoother the piece, the better the camera will work.

4. Close the flap and tape it shut so that no light can get inside.

5. Using a pin, carefully poke a tiny hole in the middle of the bottom of your box.

6. Cut off the top flaps of the box. Shape the top of the box so your face will fit snugly against it. It's a good idea to cut a space for your nose.

7. Hold the box up to your eyes and point the pinhole out the window on a sunny day. Cup your hands so that as little light gets inside as possible. You should see a miniature upside-down picture inside the box!

QUICK TIP

For your camera to work, light must enter only through the pinhole you made. If light leaks through the cracks in your box, cut up a brown paper bag and wrap it around the outside of your camera.

WHY IT WORKS

Light rays enter your box only through the pinhole. They fall on the wax paper to make a little picture or image of what's outside. Light rays travel in straight lines. Those that come from low objects outside hit near the top of the wax paper. Those from high objects outside hit near the bottom of the wax paper. So the image is upside down.

You have built a device called a camera obscura. It has been used for centuries by artists and astronomers to project images of things they wish to see.

A real camera works on the same principle. Instead of a pinhole it uses a lens which can collect a lot more light rays.

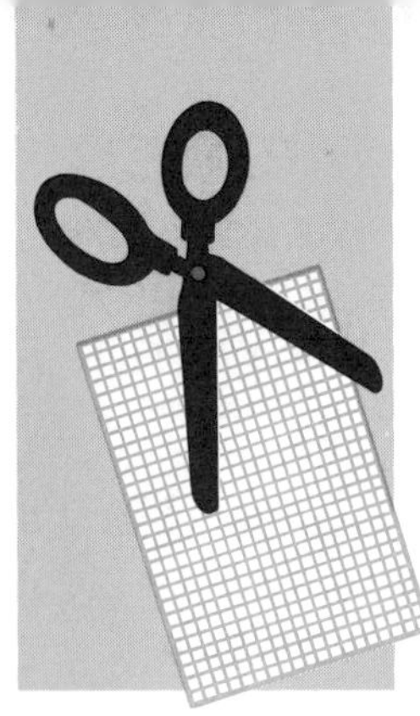

WATER WHEEL

Thousands of years ago, water wheels were invented as a way to put the power of water to good use. They're still used today.

Here's a way to make your own water wheel.

MATERIALS

Cardboard
Plastic egg cartons
String
Pencil
Ruler
Eraser
Scissors

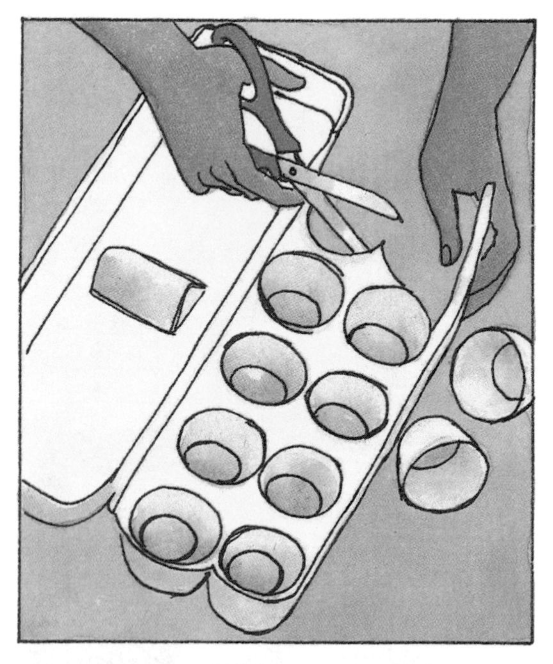

WHAT YOU DO

1. Cut out two 8-inch circles of cardboard. With the tip of your pencil, make a hole in the center of each piece of cardboard.

2. Cut up the egg cartons so that you have 12 cups or buckets.

3. Staple or tape the buckets between the pieces of cardboard. Space the buckets evenly as shown in the picture.

4. When the wheel is together, stick one of the pencils through the center holes. This is your axle.

5. Loop a string on either end of the pencil. Make the loops loose enough to let the pencil spin around.

6. Tie the other ends of the strings to the ruler.

Your water wheel is complete. Hang the buckets under a water faucet. After a few test runs, you should have it spinning smoothly.

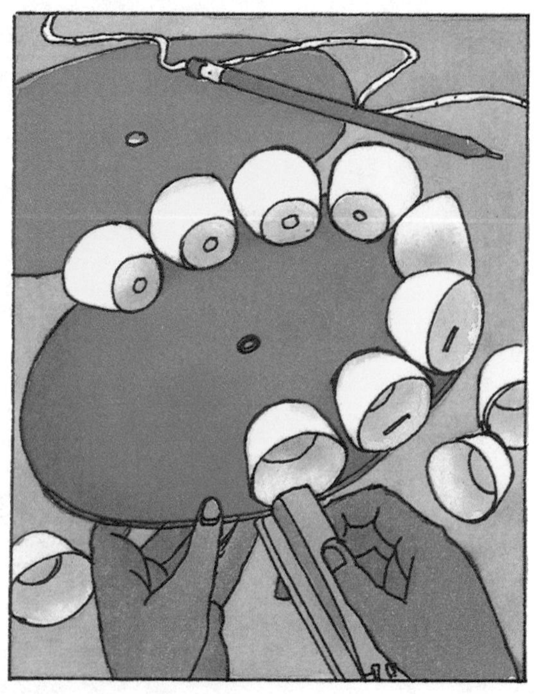

WHY IT WORKS

A water wheel harnesses the power of moving water. The force of the water pushing down the buckets causes the axle to turn. On real water wheels, the movement of the axle is strong enough to turn a grindstone or to lift heavy objects.

CRYSTAL FARM

You can start your very own crystal farm. It's easy to grow these fascinating formations in an ordinary jar.

MATERIALS

Glass jar
A bowl
A long piece of string or thread
A paper clip
A spoon
Salt
Hot water
A pencil

WHAT YOU DO

1. Turn on the hot water faucet and let the water run until it gets hot. Then carefully fill the jar.

2. Put a few teaspoons of salt into the water and stir until it has dissolved. Put in some more salt and stir again.

3. Place the jar in a bowl of very hot water. This will keep the water in the jar from cooling off. Add some more salt to the water in the jar and stir again. Keep stirring in salt until the water becomes cloudy.

4. Tie a paper clip to one end of the string or thread. Tie the other end onto a pencil. Place the pencil over the top of the jar so the paper clip hangs in the water.

5. Leave the jar for a few days. Each day you'll see the crystals get larger.

6. Look at your crystals with a magnifying glass. You'll see that each little crystal has the same shape.

QUICK TIP

Some table salt will leave the water cloudy. For best results, use a pure salt, such as kosher salt.

WHY IT WORKS

Salt is made up of tiny crystals. When you mix the salt in the hot water, these crystals dissolve, or break away from each other. The hotter your water, the more salt you can dissolve.

But as the water starts to cool, the salt crystals become attached to each other again. They group together on the paper clip, and you have your formation.

BOTTLE FOUNTAIN

Some surprising things can be done by using everyday objects in new ways. Here's an example of how you can turn a soda bottle, a drinking straw, and some clay into your own fountain.

MATERIALS

Soda bottle
Drinking straw
Modeling clay
Toothpick or straight pin
Large bowl or sink

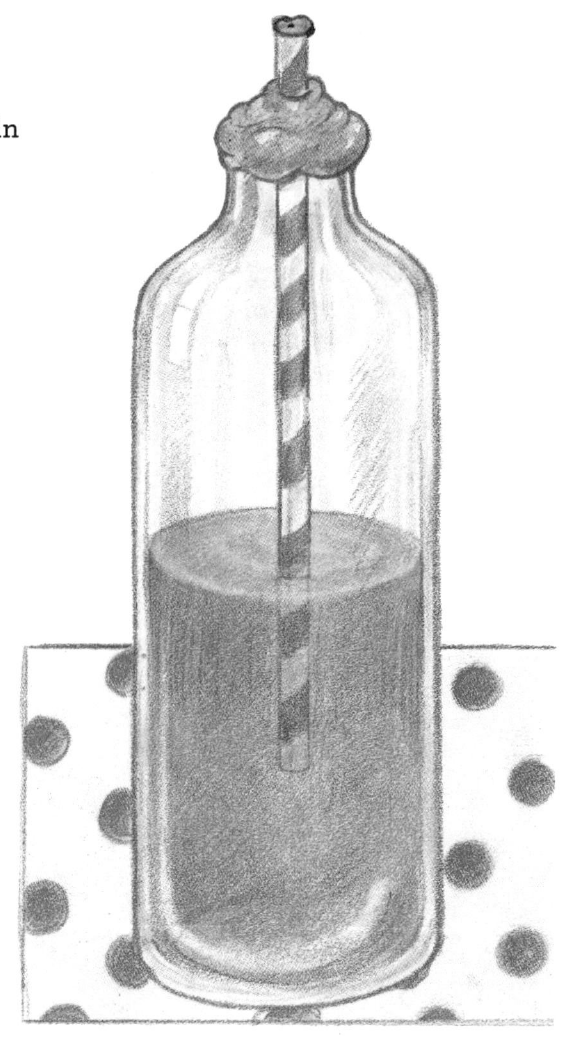

WHAT YOU DO

1. Take the cap off the soda bottle. An empty, washed-out vinegar bottle also works well. Fill the bottle halfway with very cold water.

2. Put the straw in the bottle. Press clay around the straw to hold it in place and to seal up the top of the bottle.

3. Now, plug up the top opening of the straw with clay. Then, carefully use a toothpick or a pin to make a tiny opening in the clay plug.

4. Fill up a sink or large bowl with hot water. Stand the bottle in the hot water and hold it steady.

5. Wait a few moments, and get ready to watch your fountain rise.

For a more spectacular fountain, try adding a few drops of food coloring to the water in the bottle.

WHY IT WORKS

When air is heated, it expands to take up more space. The hot water in the bowl heats up the air in the bottle. As the warm air inside the bottle expands, it pushes on the water and forces it to shoot up through the straw.

HOMEMADE ICE CREAM

Everyone loves ice cream. Here's your chance to make some from scratch.

MATERIALS

1 tablespoon of unflavored gelatin
¼ cup of hot tap water
2 cups of milk
1 can of evaporated milk
3 tablespoons of vanilla extract
½ cup of honey
A big mixing bowl
Measuring spoons and cups

WHAT YOU DO

Before you start, ask your parents if it is all right to turn the temperature down in your freezer. Look inside the freezer for a dial and turn it to the coldest possible setting.

1. Put the gelatin in a large mixing bowl. Add the hot water and stir until the gelatin dissolves.

2. Add the honey and 1 cup of milk. Stir until the honey blends with the liquid. If your milk is very cold, the gelatin will form lumps. So leave the cup of milk out of the refrigerator for a half hour before starting. Or ask a parent to warm it a bit.

3. Now add the second cup of milk. Add a cup of evaporated milk and the vanilla. Mix everything well and then place your mixing bowl in the freezer.

4. Wait one hour and then check the mixture. Is it partially frozen? Then go to Step 5. If not, put it back for a half hour. Keep doing this until the mixture is partially frozen.

5. Take out your bowl and mix the contents with an egg beater or electric mixer until fluffy.

6. Put your bowl back in the freezer for another two hours. Then take it out, grab a spoon, and start eating!

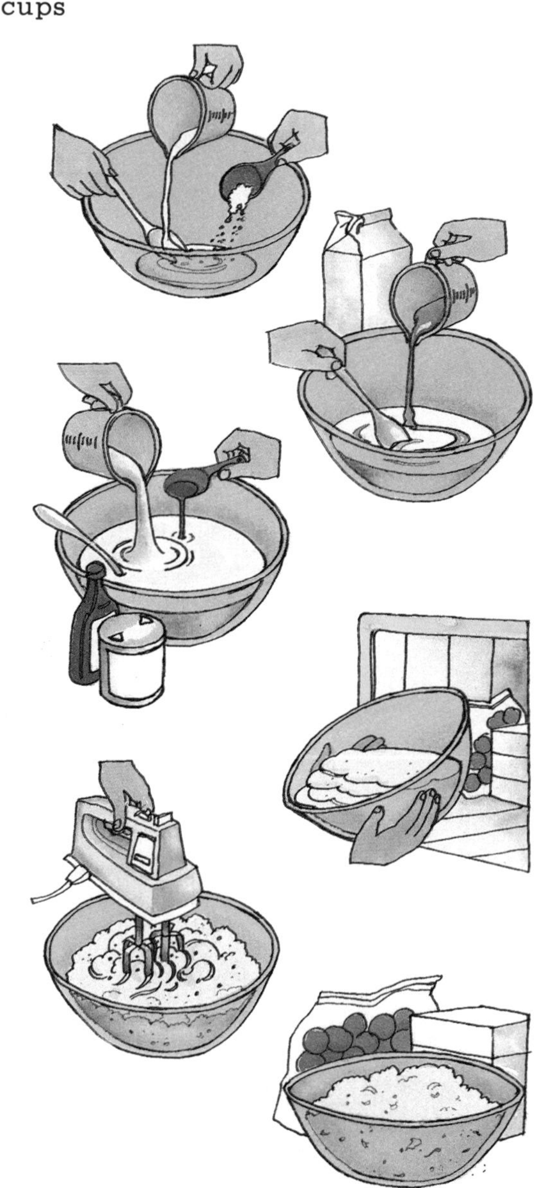

WHY IT WORKS

It takes a lower temperature to freeze ice cream than to freeze water. By turning down the thermostat in your freezer, you made it cold enough to make ice cream. (By the way, did you remember to turn it back to normal when you were finished?)

Ice cream also needs stabilizers. These chemicals keep everything well mixed and prevent ice crystals from forming. In store-bought ice cream, ingredients like guär gum and carrageenin act as stabilizers. For your ice cream, gelatin did the job.

Finally, in order to have the right texture, ice cream needs air. When you mixed your ice cream in Step 5, you fluffed it up with air.

Making ice cream is tricky. If your ice cream did not come out right, don't worry. The tasty mixture you have made will still make a great frozen dessert.

TRY THIS

Now that you've got the hang of it, make some more ice cream. This time, swirl in chocolate sauce or chopped nuts when you reach Step 5.

MAKE A PERISCOPE

A periscope will let you see over and under things and around corners—without anyone seeing *you.*

MATERIALS

One empty aluminum foil or plastic wrap box
Masking tape
Two small 2-inch by 3-inch mirrors
White glue
Scissors

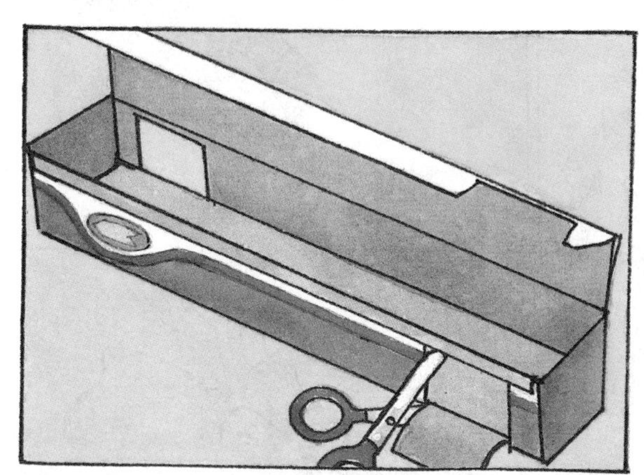

WHAT YOU DO

1. Put masking tape over the sharp cutting edge on the box. This is for your protection.

2. Cut a hole near the end of the front side of the box (see the drawing). It should be about 1½ inches long and almost as wide as the box.

3. Cut the same size hole at the back of the opposite end of the box.

4. Place the mirrors in the box as shown in the drawing. Their reflecting surfaces should face into the center of the box.

5. Tape the mirrors temporarily into place. Then close the box and try out your periscope. Look through one end. Can you see what is around the corner? If not, adjust the mirror positions until you can see through the box.

6. When the mirrors are in the right position, tape or glue them into place. Then tape the box shut. Decorate the outside of your periscope with wrapping paper or colorful stars and other shapes.

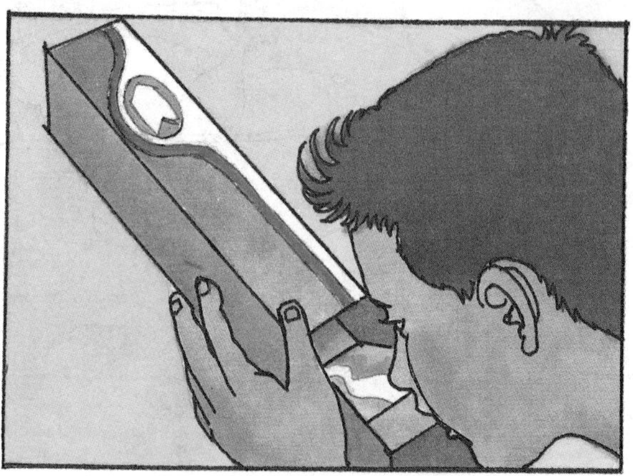

Your periscope will work best if you use an 18-inch box.

WHY IT WORKS

While you look in one end of the periscope, light reflects off objects and enters the other end. The light bounces off one mirror and then the other. Finally, it reaches your eye and you can see what is happening around the corner.

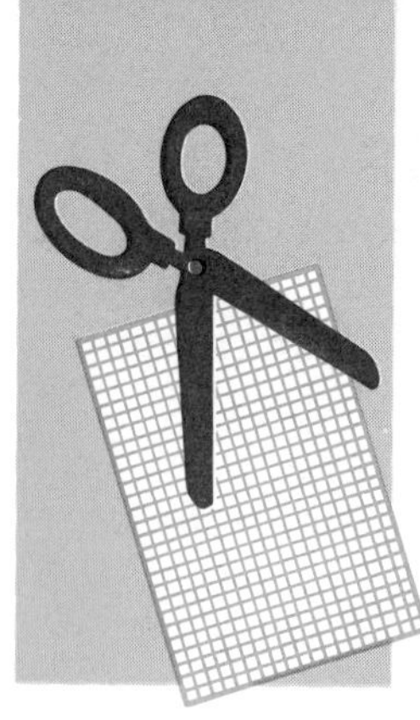

DIVING SUBMARINE

You can turn a soda bottle into a submarine. It will dive underwater and rise to the surface—at your command!

MATERIALS

Plastic soda bottle
Pencil
Six quarters
Transparent tape
Two straws
Modeling clay

WHAT YOU DO

1. Use the pencil carefully to make five holes in the side of the bottle. The holes should line up between the top and bottom of the bottle.

2. Tape three quarters on each side of the holes. The picture on the next page shows you where to tape the coins. The quarters serve as weights and will keep the side of the bottle with the holes facing downward.

3. Fit the end of one straw into the end of the other. Tape them together.

4. Put the straws into the bottle opening and plug up the rest of the opening with clay. Bend the tip of the straw so it points upward when it's inside the bottle. This will help keep water from coming into the straw.

5. Float your submarine in a sink or tub full of water. You are ready for your first test dive.

6. Suck the air out of the bottle through the straw. The submarine will dive to the bottom. To bring your sub back to the surface, just blow air through the straws—your craft will rise.

Tape your coins like this.

WHY IT WORKS

A real submarine has tanks that make it float and sink. When the tanks are filled with water, the added weight sinks the boat. When the tanks are filled with air, the boat becomes lighter and rises to the surface.

Your bottle works the same way. When you suck out the air, water fills the bottle and it sinks. When you blow air back into the bottle, it floats.

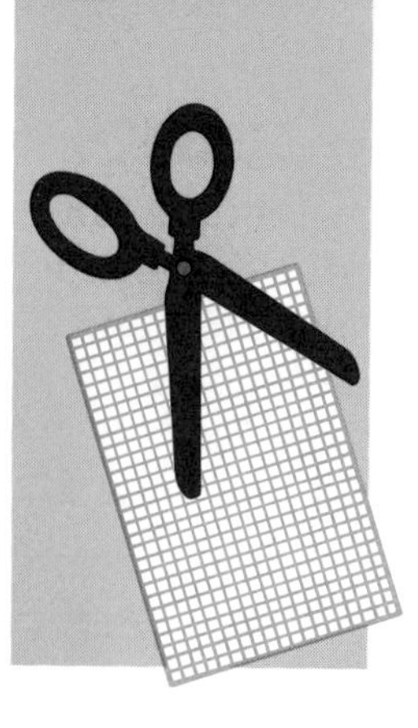

THE RAINING JAR

Here's a way to make it rain without getting wet.

MATERIALS

Glass jar (without the lid)
Pie tin
Ice cubes
Hot water

WHAT YOU DO

1. Place the pie tin in the freezer until it gets icy cold. Then take it out and fill it with ice cubes.

2. Just before you take the pie tin out of the freezer, carefully fill the jar with hot tap water.

3. Place the pie tin over the jar's mouth. Let it sit there for a few minutes.

4. Watch what happens inside the jar. The sides of the jar will become cloudy and wet, as if a storm is brewing in there. Soon it will begin to rain.

5. After a few more minutes, lift up the pie tin. Watch the "rain" that has formed on the bottom of the tin drop into the jar.

WHY IT WORKS

Water is not always liquid. When it freezes, it turns into solid ice. In the air around you, water is a gas or "vapor."

The hot water in the jar turns into vapor. It rises until it hits the bottom of the cold pie tin. There, the cold surface turns the vapor back into a liquid. The drops hang on the tin until they get too heavy and fall.

When vapor changes into liquid water, it "condenses." Clouds are made of vapor that has condensed into droplets. Rain falls when many little droplets form large, heavy drops.

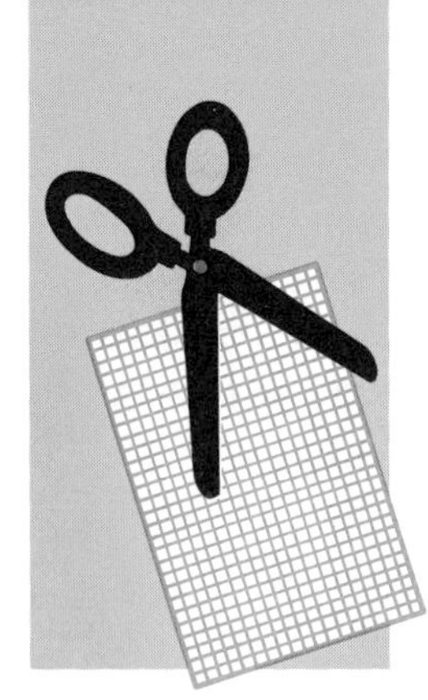

KITCHEN GOO

Cornstarch is used to thicken soups and stews. You can use it to make a strange gooey mixture.

MATERIALS

2 small bowls
A tablespoon
1 box of cornstarch
1 small spoon for stirring
Water

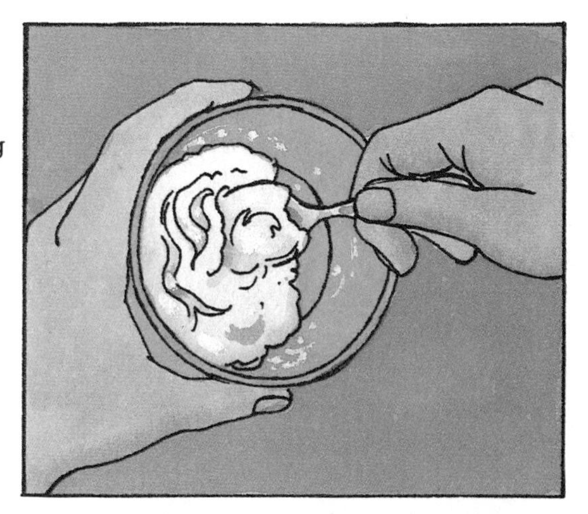

WHAT YOU DO

1. Put two tablespoons of water into a bowl. Dry off the tablespoon.

2. Slowly stir one tablespoon of cornstarch into the water.

3. Add another tablespoon of cornstarch and stir it in slowly. Make sure to break up any lumps that form.

4. Slowly stir in a third tablespoon of cornstarch.

5. The liquid will start to do odd things now. Try to stir it quickly. Is it hard to push the spoon through the mixture? Now stir slowly. Does the liquid flow smoothly again? If it doesn't, add some more cornstarch—a little bit at a time. Put in more water if your goo is too thick to stir.

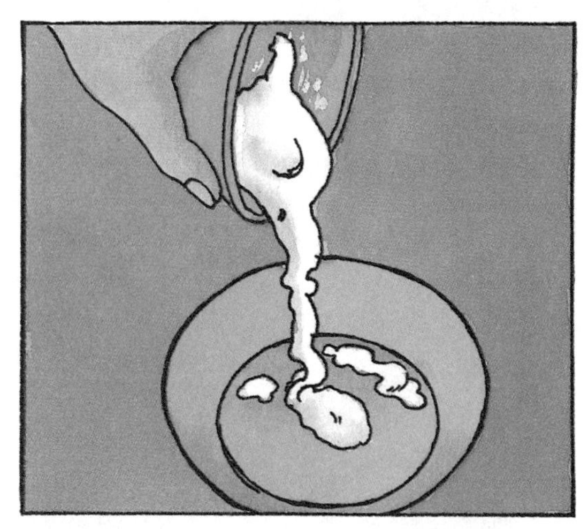

6. Pour the liquid into the second small bowl. Does it look thick and curly as you pour it?

7. Hold a spoon a few inches above your bowl of goo. Watch what happens when you drop the spoon. Let part of the spoon sink. Then, try to pull the spoon out quickly—but be careful. You will find that the spoon lifts the whole bowl before it slips out of the liquid.

8. Stick your fingers in the concoction and squeeze it. Let it run between your fingers. What a gooey sensation!

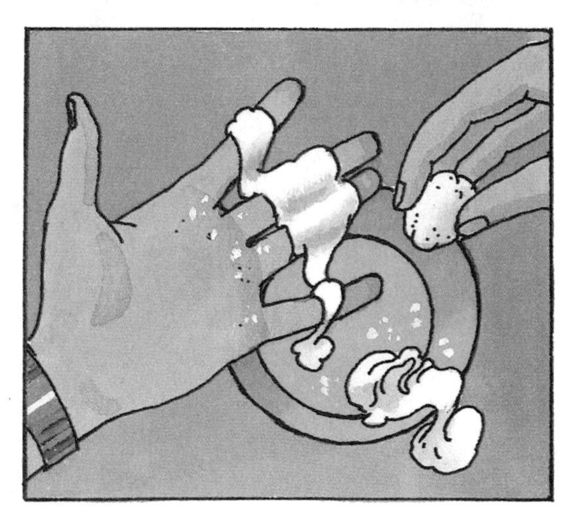

QUICK TIP

The trick to getting your mixture to behave strangely is to combine just the right amounts of water and cornstarch. Give it a few tries.

WHY IT WORKS

Your mixture behaves so strangely because cornstarch is made up of lots of tiny coarse grains, almost like fine sand. The water forms a thin film around the grains. When you stir very slowly, the grains easily slide smoothly past each other. But when you stir quickly or push hard, the grains become packed tightly and form an almost solid mass.

BOTTLE THERMOMETER

You can make a thermometer that really works.

MATERIALS

Glass bottle with small mouth
Straw
Modeling clay
3 x 5 index card or piece of cardboard
Red food coloring
Eyedropper
Tape
Weather thermometer
Warm water
Marker or pen

WHAT YOU DO

1. Fill the bottle all the way to the top with warm water. Add some red food coloring to the water.

2. Put the straw into the water in the bottle. Mold clay firmly around the straw and the mouth of the bottle. Seal the bottle tightly with the clay.

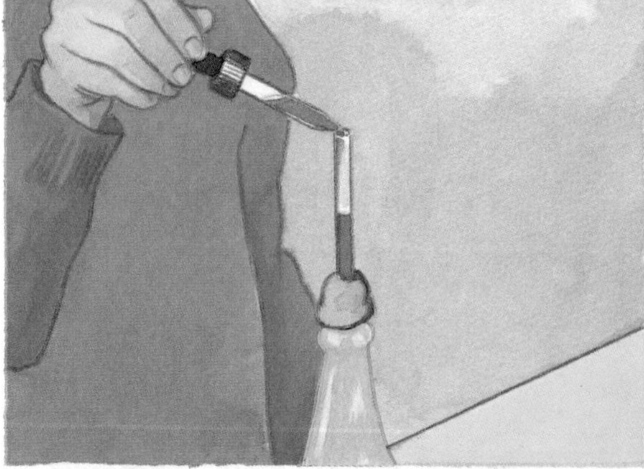

3. Add a small amount of warm red-colored water through the top of the straw with an eyedropper. Stop when the water level in the straw is about an inch above the top of the bottle.

4. Plug the top end of the straw with a tiny stopper made of clay.

5. Tape the index card sideways onto the straw as you see in the picture. Draw a straight line on the card to mark the level of the water in the straw.

6. Check the bottle thermometer two or three hours later. Mark the level again. Check the temperature on the outdoor thermometer. Write the temperature on the card next to the line you drew.

7. Keep checking and marking over the next few days. Soon you will have a range of markings and numbers. You can now use your bottle thermometer to check the temperature.

WHY IT WORKS

When the air becomes warmer, it warms the water in the thermometer. Water takes up more space when it is warm. In this case it moves up into the straw because there is nowhere else for it to go in the tightly sealed bottle. When the air cools down, the water cools down, too. It "shrinks," or contracts. Now it takes up less room. The water in the straw moves back down into the bottle.

STUMPER

Your thermometer uses water to measure temperature. Most store-bought thermometers use mercury or alcohol. Can you guess why? What would happen to your thermometer if the temperature dropped below 32°F?

KALEIDOSCOPE FUN

When you look through a kaleidoscope, you see amazing, changing patterns of color. With a few simple materials, you can make your own kaleidoscope.

MATERIALS

3 wallet-sized mirrors of the same size
Tape
A piece of white cardboard
A pencil
Scissors
Colored paper or beads
A lamp

WHAT YOU DO

1. Tape the three mirrors together to form a triangle. The reflecting surfaces should face inward. This will be the body of the kaleidoscope.

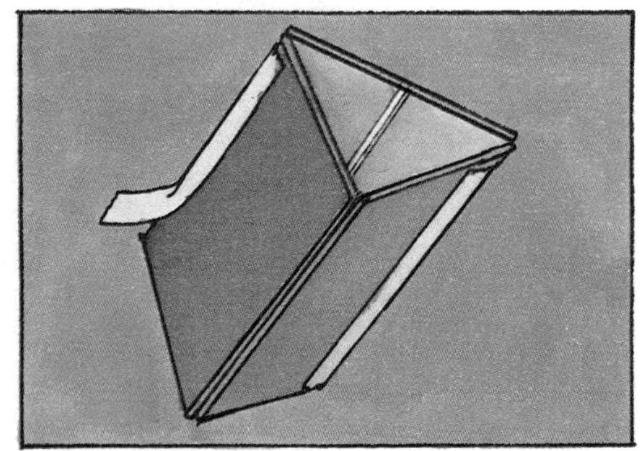

2. Set the mirrors on end on the cardboard. Trace a triangle to form the kaleidoscope's bottom.

3. Cut out the cardboard base and tape it to one end of the kaleidoscope body.

4. Cut up a few small bits of colored paper or gather some small beads. Drop them into the kaleidoscope. Then place it over a lamp. Look inside. Do you see a pattern? Shake the kaleidoscope. How does the pattern change?

QUICK TIP

Variety stores and drug stores are good places to find mirrors that work best for your kaleidoscope.

WHY IT WORKS

The reflection from the colored paper or beads bounces from mirror to mirror. This creates a repeating set of patterns.

MAKE A BAROMETER

A barometer measures air pressure. Changing air pressure tells you what kind of weather to expect. Make your own barometer and see if you can become an expert at predicting the weather.

MATERIALS

A glass bottle or jar with a wide mouth, such as a peanut butter jar
A large balloon
Scissors
Rubber bands
A plastic straw
Glue or rubber cement
An empty milk or juice carton
An index card
Paper and pencil

WHAT YOU DO

1. Cut a piece of the balloon big enough to fit over the mouth of the jar. Stretch the piece over the jar and hold it in place with some rubber bands.

2. Glue one end of the straw to the middle of the piece of balloon.

3. Glue the index card to the side of the milk carton as shown in the picture. Place it so the straw that you glued to your jar points approximately to the middle of the card.

4. Put the jar and milk carton in a place where the temperature stays pretty much the same. Set them up so the straw points to the middle of the card. Mark that spot on the card.

5. Check your barometer every day. Write down on a piece of paper whether the straw is pointing to a higher or lower spot than the mark you made on the first day.

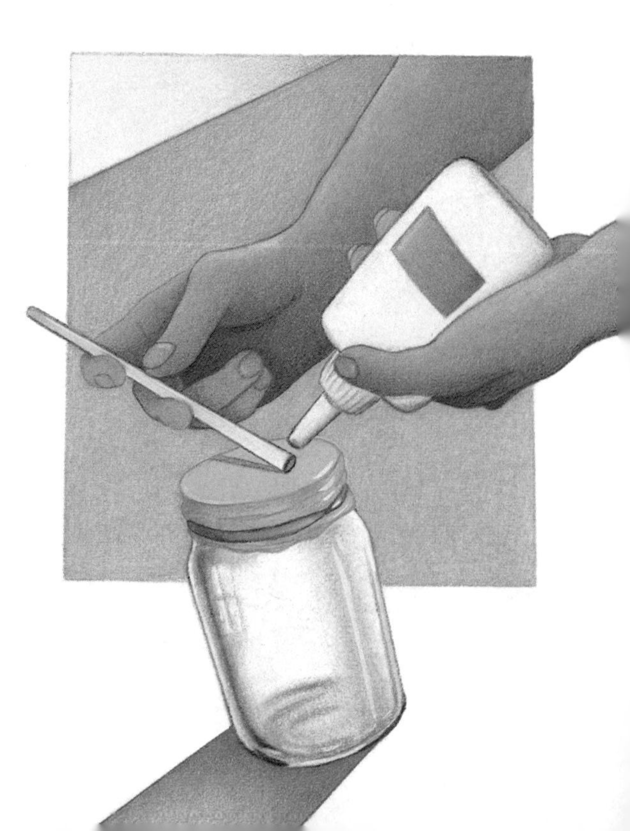

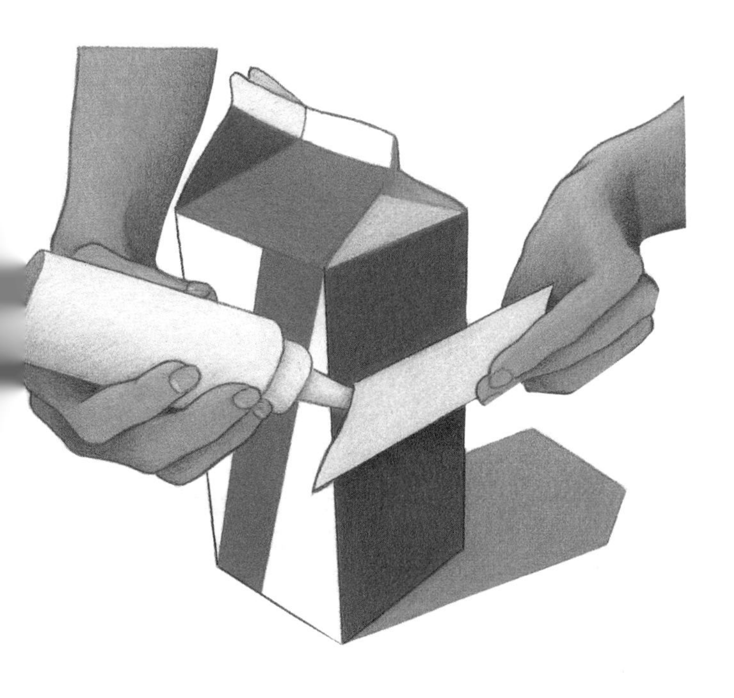

WHY IT WORKS

When you first put the balloon piece on the jar, the pressure of the air inside the jar is the same as the pressure of the air outside. When the pressure of the air outside increases, it presses down on the balloon. The end of the straw that is glued to the balloon goes down, and the other end goes up. This tells you that clear weather is ahead. When the air pressure on the outside of the jar decreases, the straw moves the other way. Stormy weather is on its way.

Air temperature will affect your results. That's why it's important to keep your barometer in a place where the temperature doesn't change very much.

QUICK TIP

From time to time, you must balance the air pressure on your barometer. After three days, remove the balloon so air can get in and out of the jar. Then attach the balloon and your barometer will work again.

FREEZING THE ACTION

The colored wheel on the opposite page is a stroboscope. By looking through it, you can make fast-moving objects seem like they're standing still.

MATERIALS

A pencil with an eraser
A pushpin or thumbtack
Scissors
Paper-thin cardboard

WHAT YOU DO

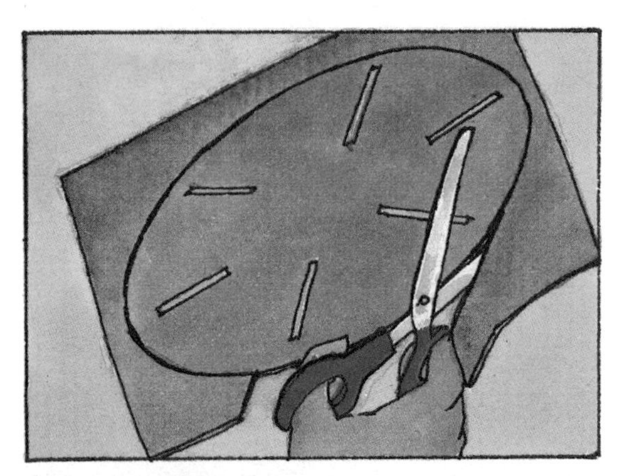

1. Trace the stroboscope wheel onto a piece of paper and cut it out. Then place the cutout wheel on a piece of thin cardboard.

2. Cut around the wheel with scissors.

3. Cut out the area of each of the slits in the cardboard wheel.

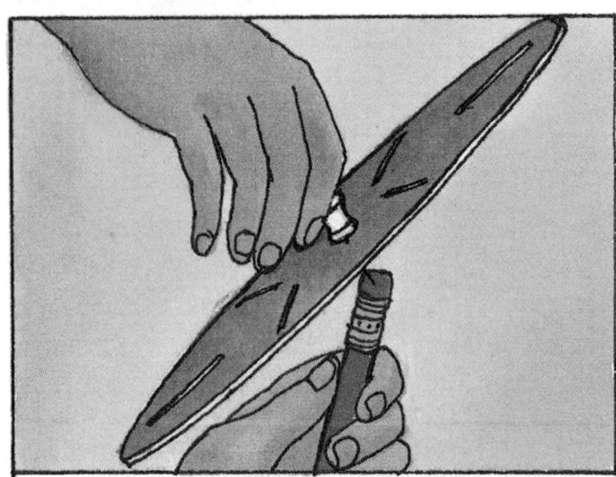

4. Carefully poke a pushpin or thumbtack through the center of the wheel. Stick the pushpin or thumbtack into the pencil eraser, as shown in the drawing. The disk should spin freely. You now have a stroboscope.

5. Spin the strobe at a steady speed. It must not wobble. Look through it at objects like spinning records and turning bike wheels, or a fast-dripping stream of water from a faucet. The objects will seem to stand still or to move slowly—depending on the strobe's speed.

QUICK TIPS

The strobe works better if the moving objects are brightly lit. Remember, it will take a little practice to spin the strobe steadily. It will also take some practice to spin the strobe at the exact speed to stop action. Be sure to try your strobe at different speeds.

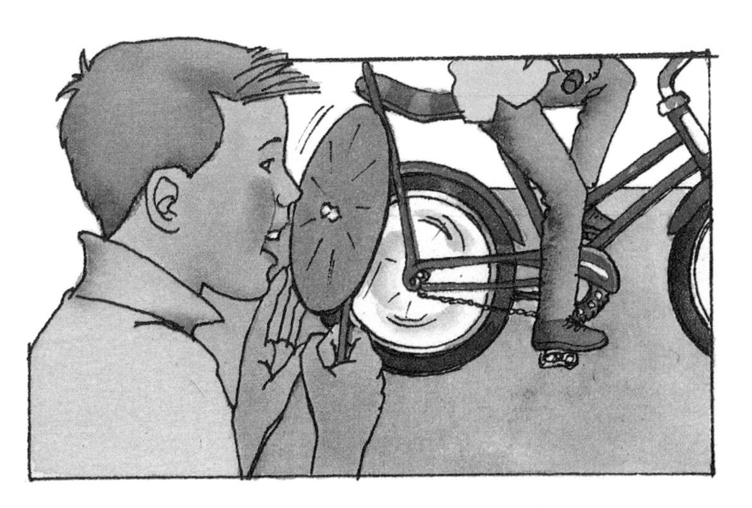

WHY IT WORKS

When objects move fast, you often can't see them. For example, you can't see the spinning spokes on a fast-moving bike wheel.

Your strobe seems to slow things down. As you spin it, light reaches your eyes in steady bursts. It's as if your eyes see a group of still photos. Spin it at the right speed, and you see one picture again and again. The object seems to be standing still.

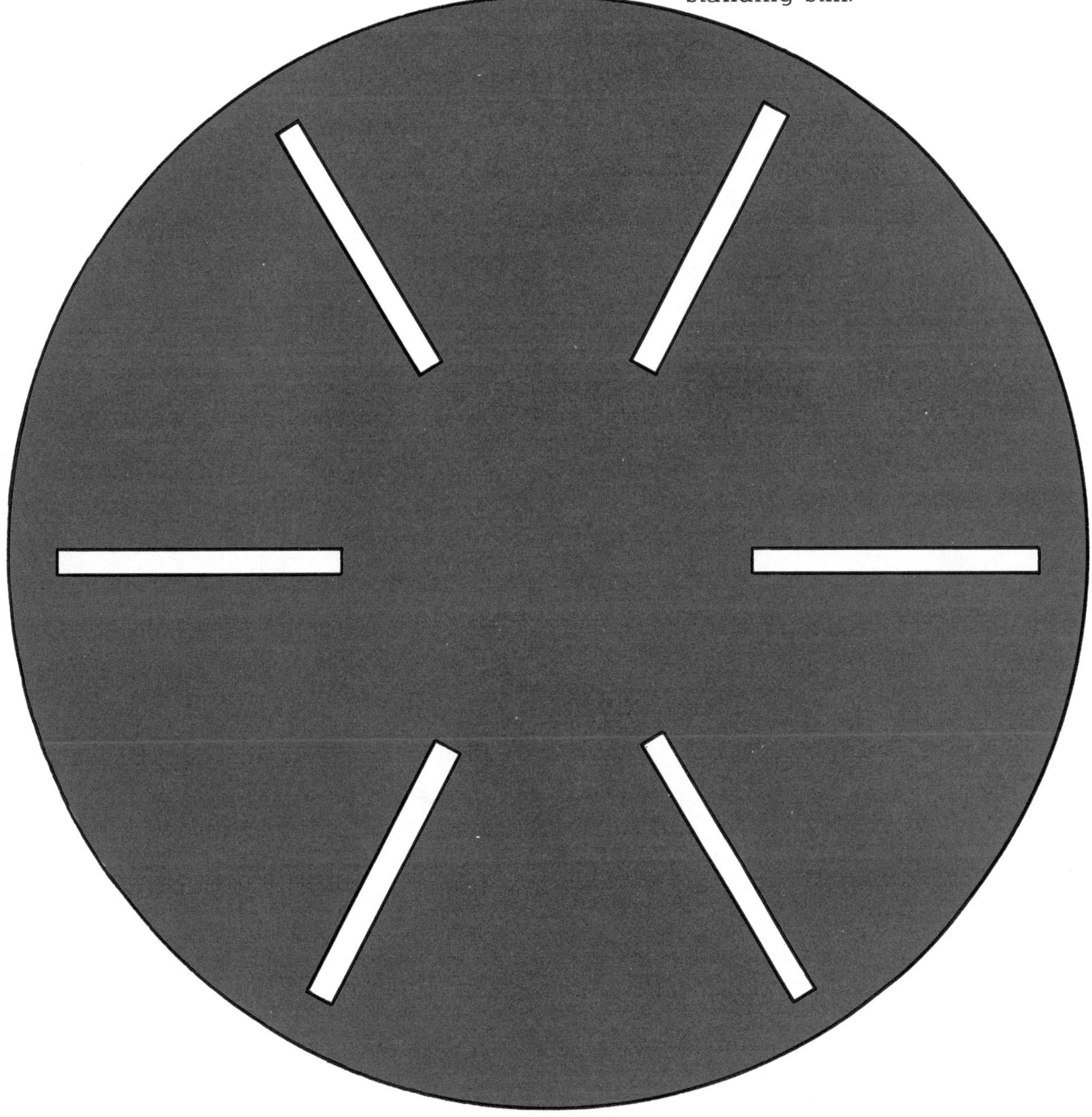

TRASH BAG KITE

Not only are kites a lot of fun, but they are also a great way to see the effects of wind currents. You can easily make a kite from a few things you have around the house.

MATERIALS

A light-colored plastic garbage bag (kitchen size)
4 plastic drinking straws
Kite string
Colored felt-tipped markers
Tape
Scissors
Ruler

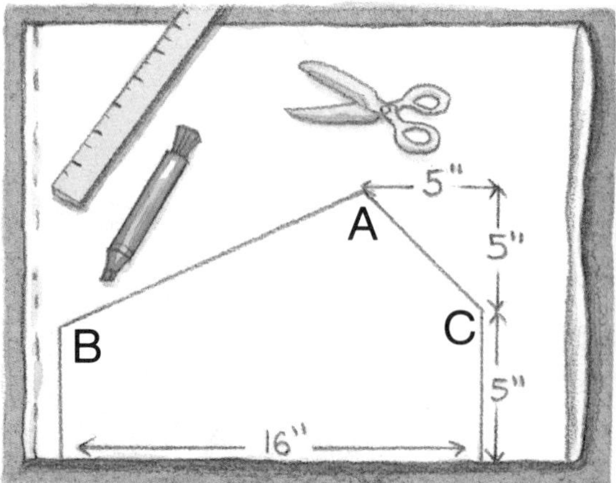

WHAT YOU DO

1. Using a marker, draw a measurement of 16 inches along the side of the bag. Draw other measurements as shown.

2. From A, draw lines to B and C to create the angles. Cut out the shape, making sure you don't cut along the side of the bag.

3. Unfold the shape and tape it to a table or flat board.

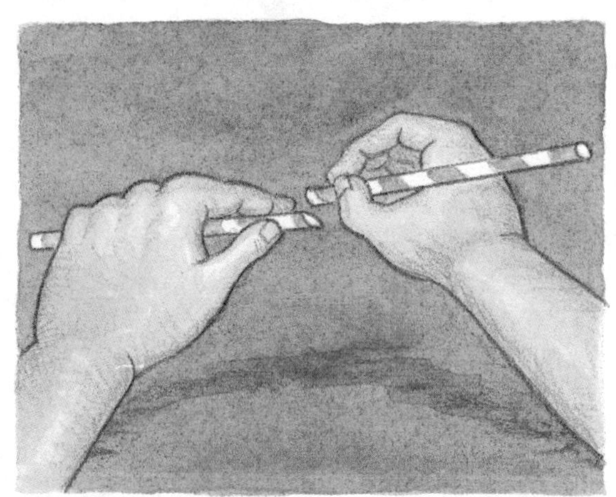

4. Pinch the end of one straw and slip it into the end of a second straw. Tape the two straws together at the spot where they meet. Repeat this step with the other two straws.

5. Tape the straws to the kite as shown in the picture. Trim the straws if they stick out farther than the edges of the kite.

6. Take off the tape holding the kite down. Put pieces of tape on the tips of the kite for reinforcement.

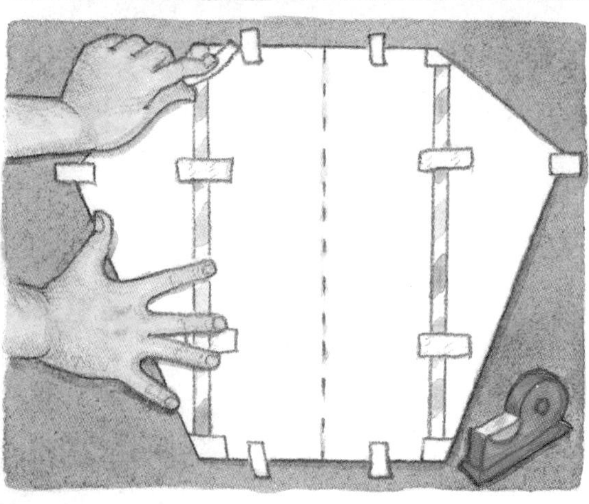

7. With the tip of the scissors, make a small hole in the two outermost tips of the kite. Tie a string through the holes. The string should be about 24 inches long. Color the kite with the markers.

8. Loop an end of the kite string to the string attached to the kite. Keep the straws on the side of the kite facing the ground. You are ready for takeoff.

WHY IT WORKS

When you hold your kite in the wind, it makes the wind turn downward. But that makes the kite go upward. Your kite moves around as it becomes caught in wind currents. To keep your kite up, tug gently on the string. That forces more of the wind down, which in turn forces your kite up.

QUICK TIP

The best place to fly a kite is a spot where a steady wind is blowing up a gradually sloping hill.

WATER MICROSCOPE

You can use water's ability to bend light to make a microscope.

MATERIALS

A large plastic container such as the kind that holds cottage cheese or yogurt
Plastic wrap
A rubber band
Scissors

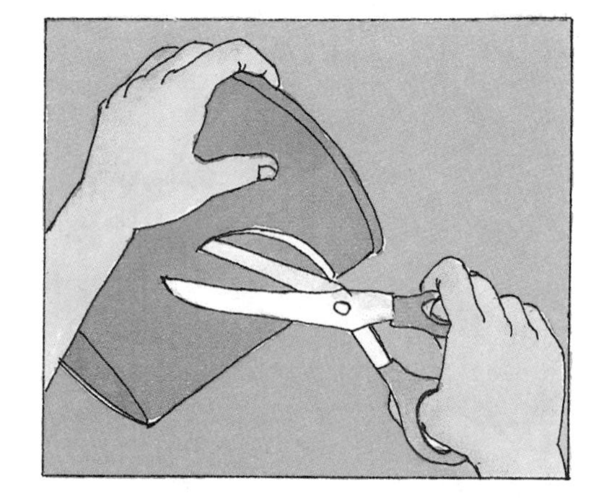

WHAT YOU DO

1. Cut a hole in the side of the container. It should be large enough to fit your fingers.

2. Stretch the plastic wrap over the top of the container. Push the plastic wrap down so that it sinks a bit in the middle. Use the rubber band to hold the plastic wrap in place.

3. Carefully pour water on top of the plastic wrap so that it forms a pool.

4. Place your fingers in the hole and look at them from above. Move them up and down until they come into focus most sharply. How do they look?

5. Look at different things through your microscope. For instance, you could look at a bit of newspaper, a comic book picture, a strand of hair, a piece of fabric, a flower petal, an onion skin, an insect, or a grain of rice. How is what you see with your microscope different from what you see with just your eyes?

WHY IT WORKS

The curve of the plastic wrap causes the water to act as a lens. The lens bends the light. This bending of the light changes the way things appear. In this case, it makes your fingers seem larger.

TRY THIS

Here is a simple way to see the magnifying power of water. Place a newspaper on a table and cover it with plastic wrap. Using a toothpick or eyedropper, place a drop of water on the newsprint. You may need to lift the plastic wrap slightly to get the drop in focus. Try different-sized drops and notice how they magnify differently. Which are better magnifiers—big drops or small ones? Which ones are the most curved?

CLAY DOUGH

Create your own clay dough, and use it to make toys, gifts, and decorations.

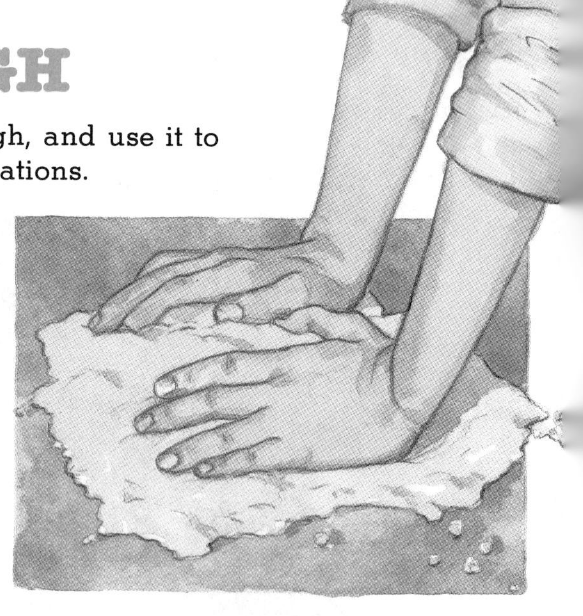

MATERIALS

1 1/2 cups of flour
1/2 cup of salt
1/2 cup of water
1/4 cup of vegetable oil
Large bowl

WHAT YOU DO

1. Mix the flour and salt together in a large bowl.

2. Slowly add the water and vegetable oil to the flour and salt. If you like, you can add a little food coloring.

3. Use your hands to knead the ingredients together. Add more flour if the dough is sticky. The clay dough is ready to use when it is well mixed and does not stick to your hands.

4. Model the clay into figures of people and animals. Flatten it and cut out shapes with cookie cutters. Make jewelry or holiday ornaments. Use a pencil to poke holes for string to run through.

5. Put your creations in a safe place for a few days and let them harden. Then you can paint them all kinds of colors.

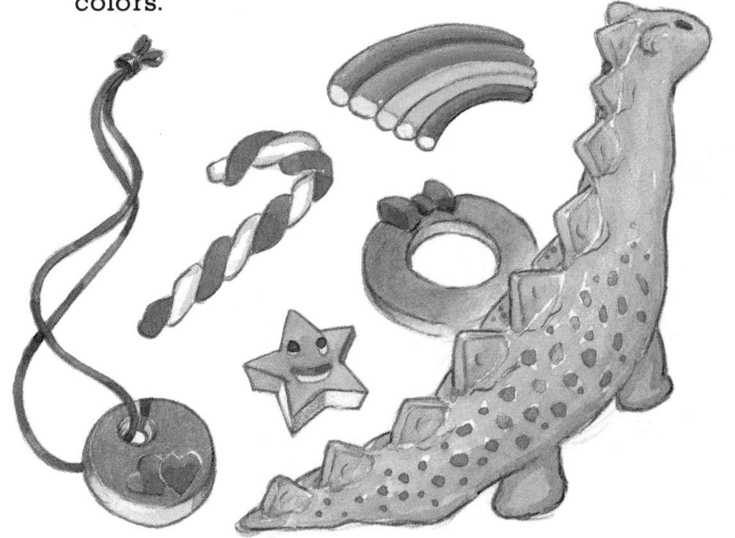

WHY IT WORKS

Adding water to flour and kneading and stirring causes a sticky substance called gluten to form. Gluten becomes stretchy and strong like clay when the right amounts of flour and water are kneaded together. And when it dries, it becomes nice and hard.

Puzzles and Fun

INVISIBLE MESSAGES

Send messages to your friends using invisible ink. Here are three ways to write secret messages using everyday items from the kitchen.

BAKING SODA CODE

Mix a teaspoon of baking soda with two teaspoons of water in a cup. Stir it well. Dip a cotton swab in the solution and write your message on white paper. Let it dry.

To make the message appear, pour a bit of purple grape juice into a cup. With a small paintbrush, paint over the paper with the message on it. Use light, even strokes from top to bottom. Your secret message will appear.

In Cabbage Detector you saw how an indicator can turn baking soda bluish green. Well, grape juice is an indicator. It causes the baking soda in your ink to turn a bluish green, and the invisible message appears.

SALTY SECRETS

You can also use water and salt to write invisible messages. Mix a tablespoon of table salt and a tablespoon of hot water in a saucer.

Use a clean cotton swab to write your message. Let the paper dry for half an hour, and your message will have disappeared.

To see the message, rub the tip of a pencil sideways over the spot where you had written your message.

MYSTERIOUS LEMONS

Still another "ink" for writing secret messages is lemon juice. Dip a toothpick into the juice and write your message.

To make the words reappear, hold the paper near a light bulb. You will be able to read what you've written. Be careful when you do this; a light bulb can get very hot.

The invisible ink reappears when it is exposed to high temperature. The paper that absorbed the lemon juice combines with oxygen in the air as the paper becomes warm. As a result, the message looks as if it was burned onto the paper.

EYEBALL BENDERS

See if your eyes can make sense of these optical illusions.

BOGGLING BOXES

Sometimes there are seven boxes here and sometimes there are eight. How many do you count?

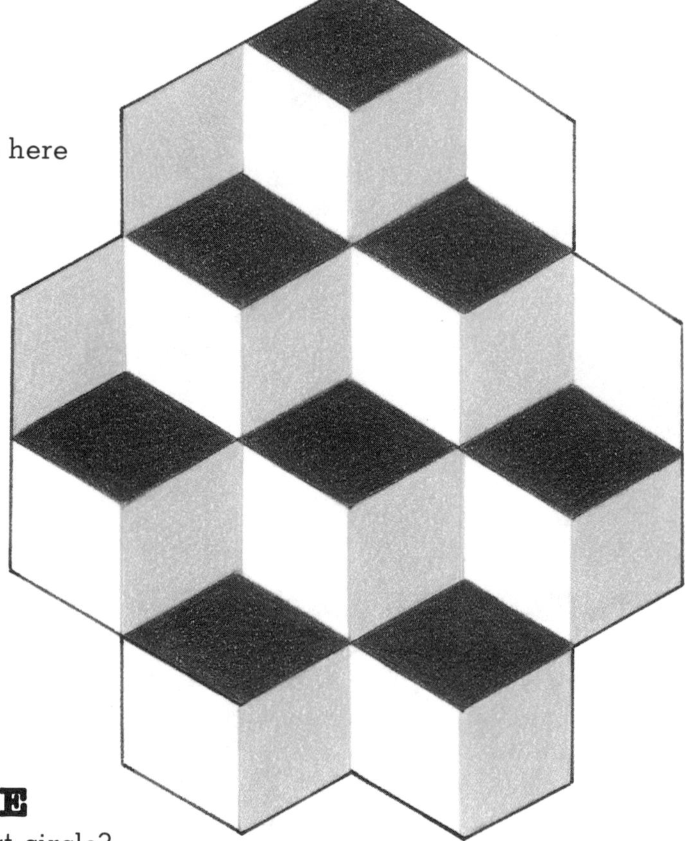

THE CROOKED CIRCLE

Is the shape you see here a perfect circle? If you think it isn't, place a coin inside it and look again.

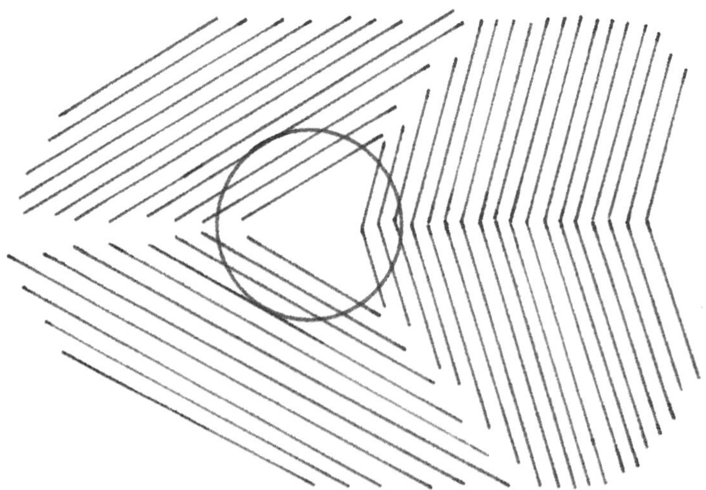

UP THE DOWN STAIRCASE

Are these stairs going up or down? If you think they go up, stare at them and turn the page slowly.

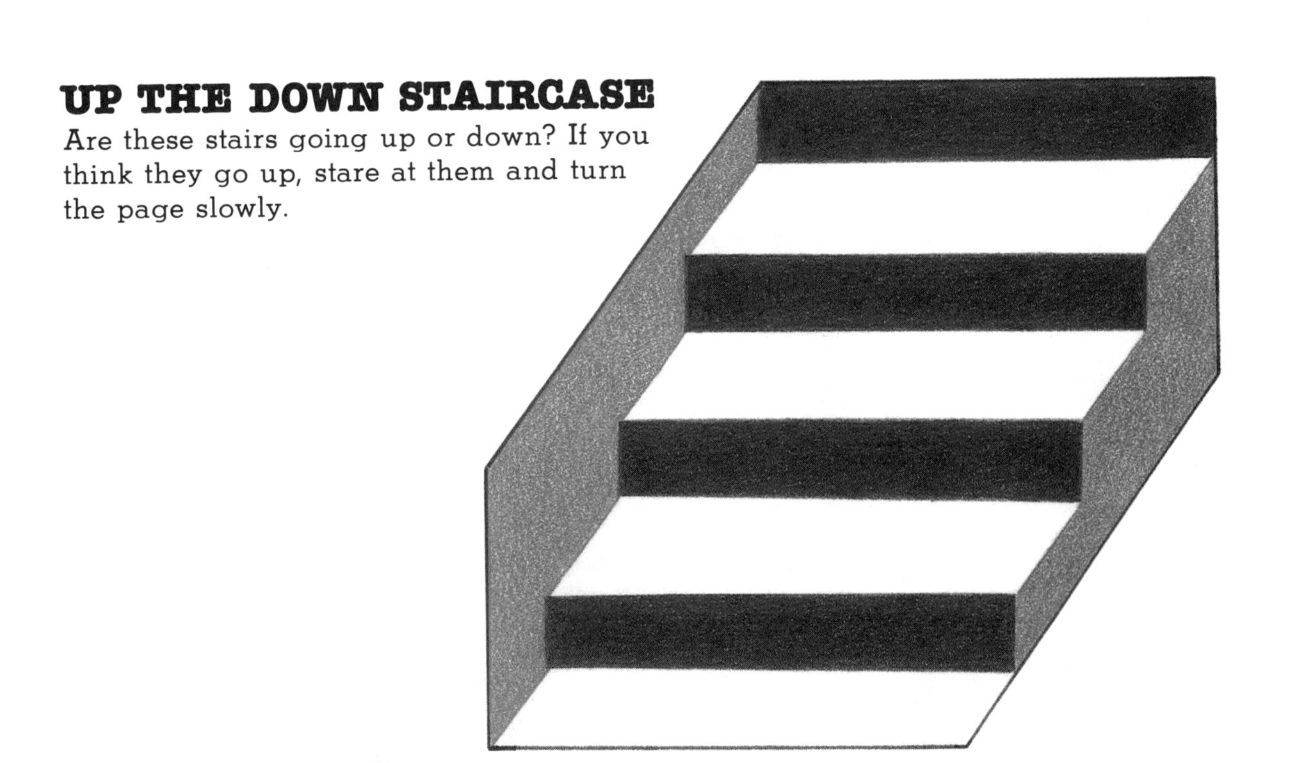

WHAT'S MY LINE?

In each pair, which line is longer—A or B?

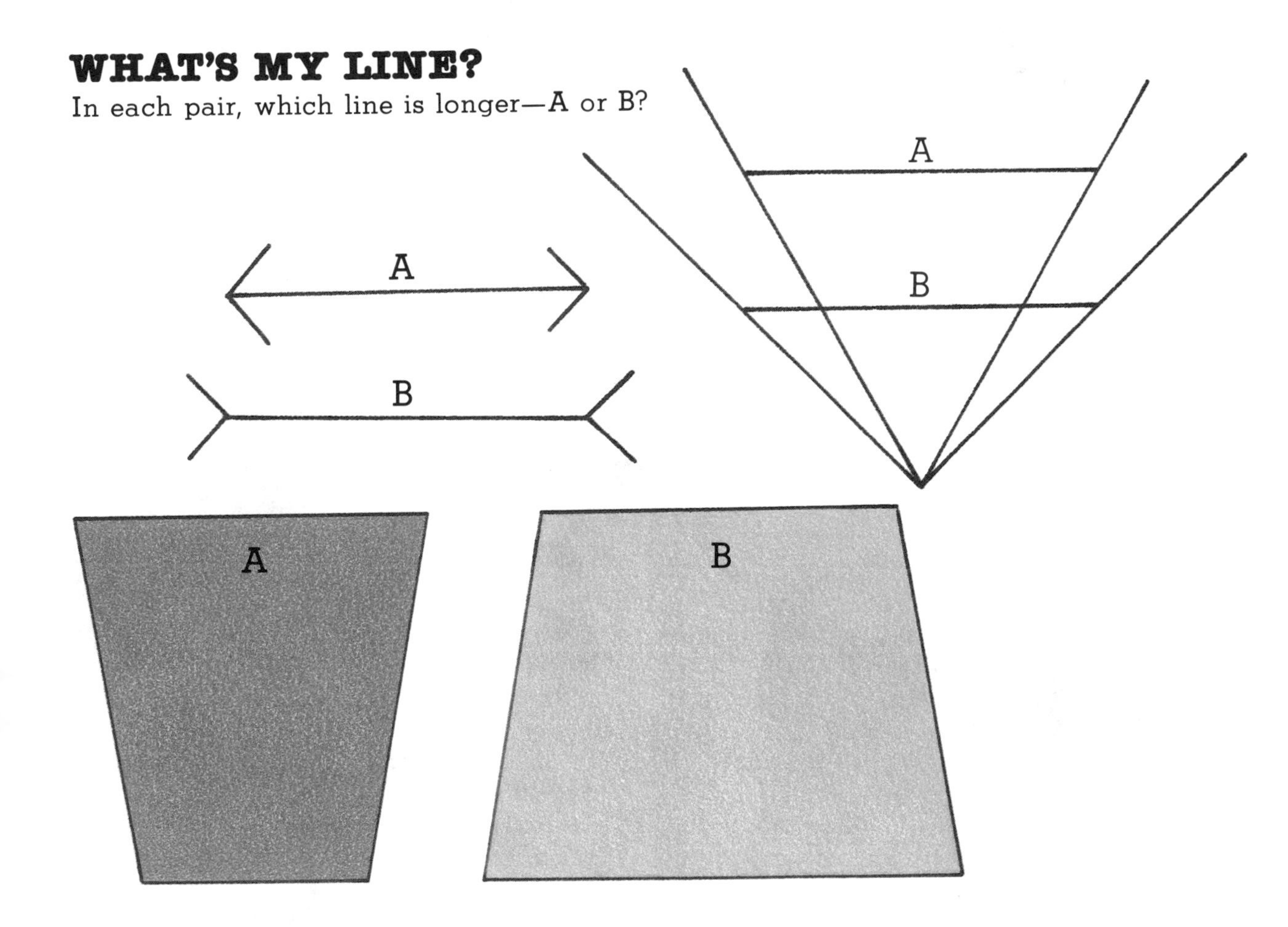

MIRROR MESSAGES

You can communicate with your friends using mysterious mirror messages.

MIRROR CODES

While looking in the mirror, write a message on a piece of paper so the message appears correct in the mirror. Now look at the message away from the mirror. Your friend will have to use a mirror to know what it says!

You can create a mysterious message without a mirror. Just try writing backwards. When you're finished, check your results in a mirror. Can you read what you wrote? When you first write mirror codes, it's easiest to use capital letters. Once you get the hang of it, you can write in upper and lower case.

Here are some messages in mirror code for you to decipher. You can make up your own, too.

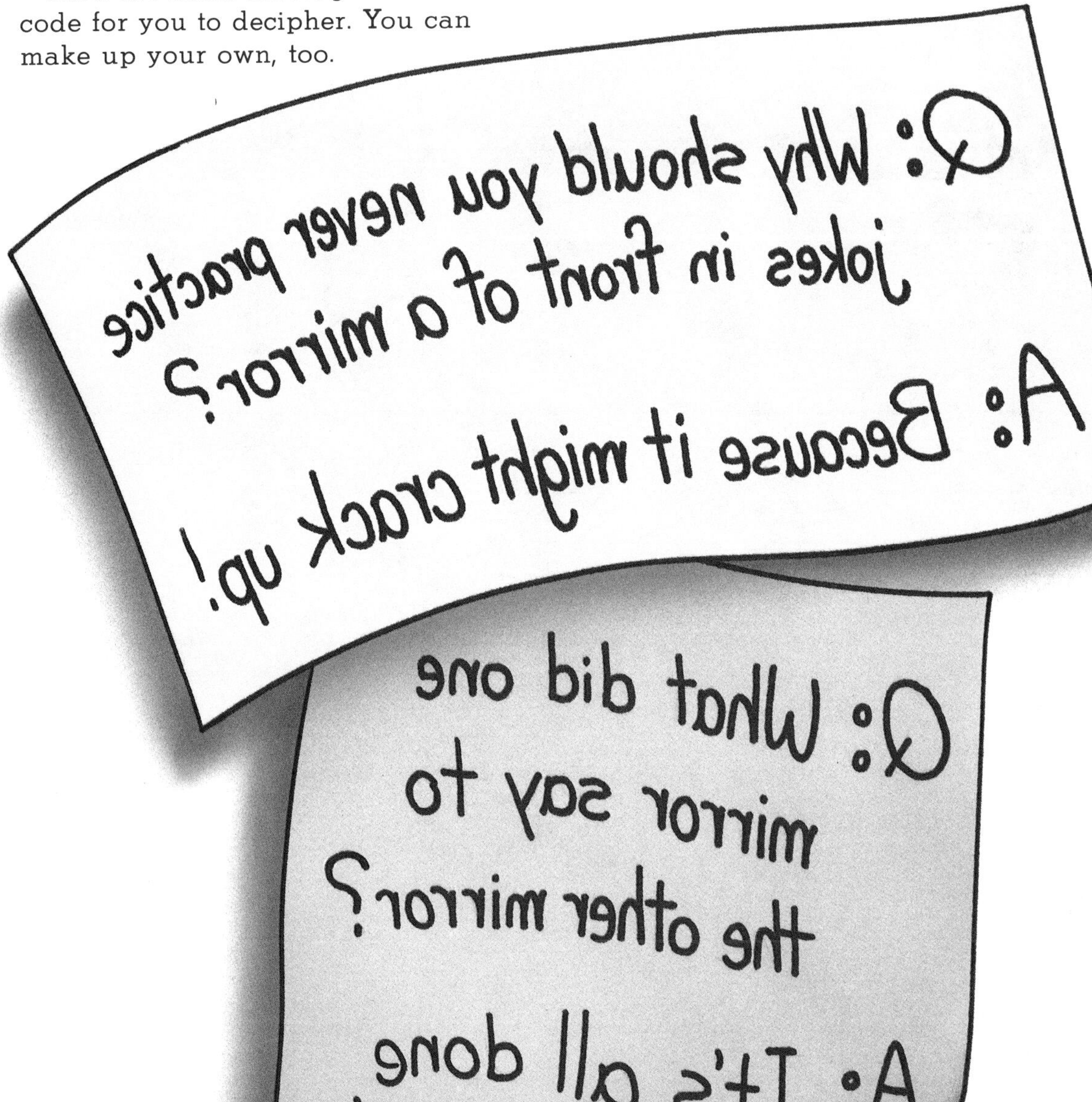

FLOATERS AND SINKERS

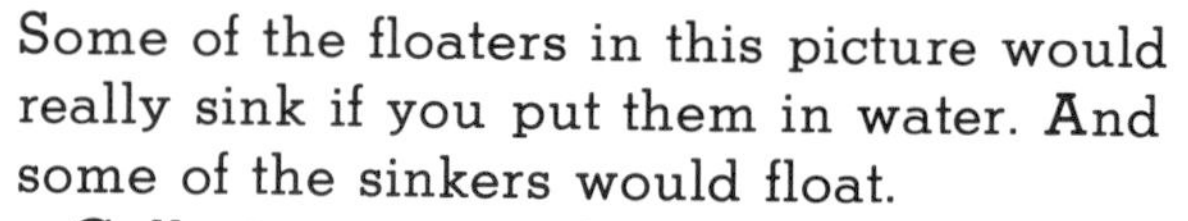

Some of the floaters in this picture would really sink if you put them in water. And some of the sinkers would float.

Collect as many of these objects as you can. Drop each one in the water and see what happens. Did you guess correctly which ones really float?

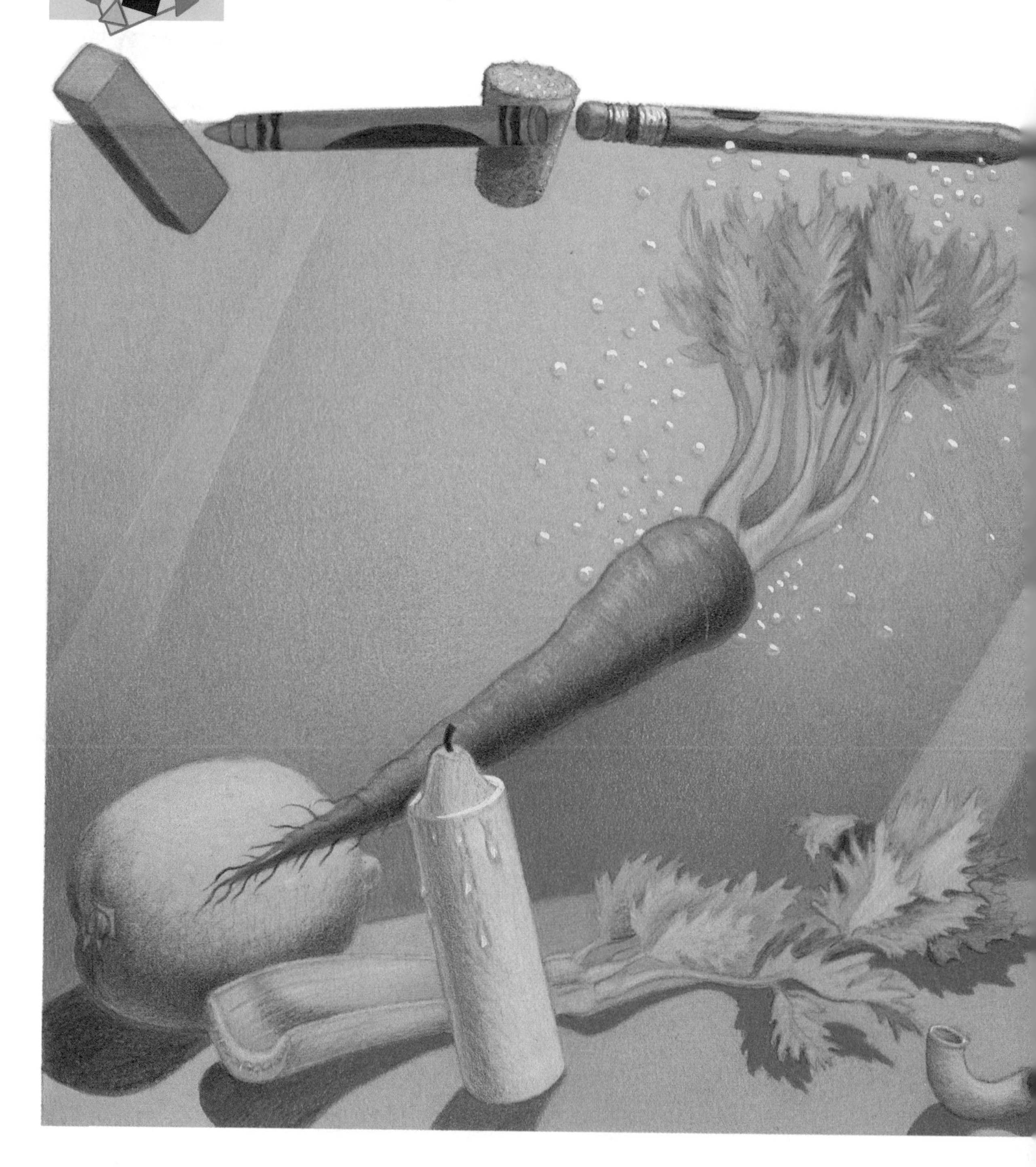

You probably think that heavy things sink and light ones float. That's often true, but it's only part of the story. The way in which weight is packed into a carrot or a coin makes a difference, too. That's why things that sometimes seem as light as a feather sink, while heavier objects sometimes float.

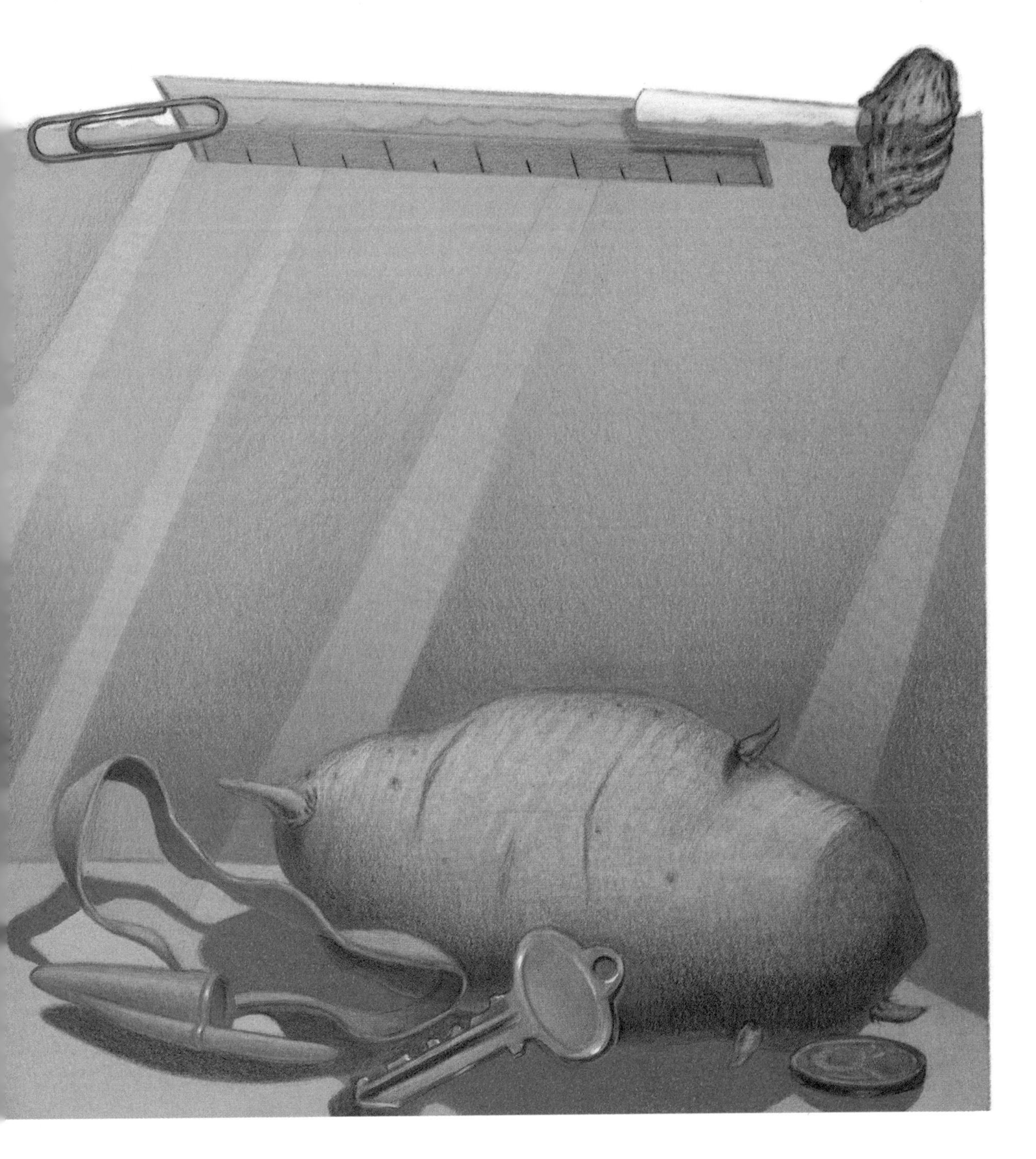

WATCH THE WIND

If you watch carefully, you can often tell how fast the wind is blowing. That's what Sir Francis Beaufort did. Nearly 200 years ago, he created a scale you can still use to measure wind speed by observing its effect on things around you.

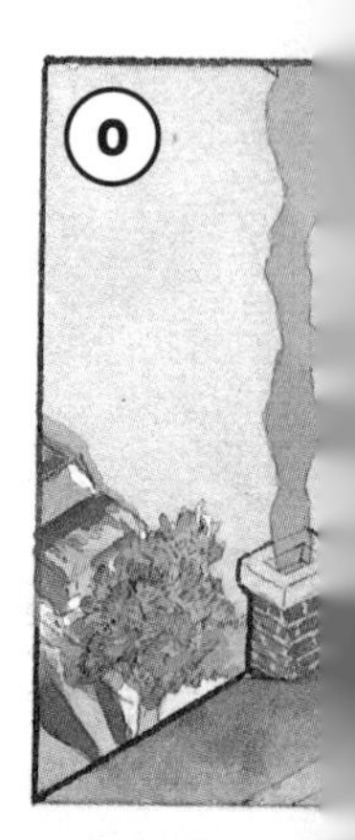

SCALE NUMBER	WIND SPEED MILES PER HOUR	THINGS YOU OBSERVE
0	**under 1**	smoke rises straight up
1	**1 to 3**	smoke drifts
2	**4 to 7**	leaves on trees rustle, you feel wind on your face
3	**8 to 12**	flags flap, paper and leaves blow along the ground
4	**13 to 18**	paper and leaves are blown into the air
5	**19 to 24**	small trees sway
6	**25 to 31**	flags flap, hats blow off, umbrellas are hard to use
7	**32 to 38**	large trees move, people have difficulty walking into wind
8	**39 to 46**	twigs snap off trees, walking into wind is nearly impossible
9	**47 to 54**	branches snap off trees, shingles fly off roofs
10	**55 to 63**	trees are uprooted, buildings are damaged
11	**64 to 75**	violent winds cause serious property damage
12	**over 75**	hurricane!

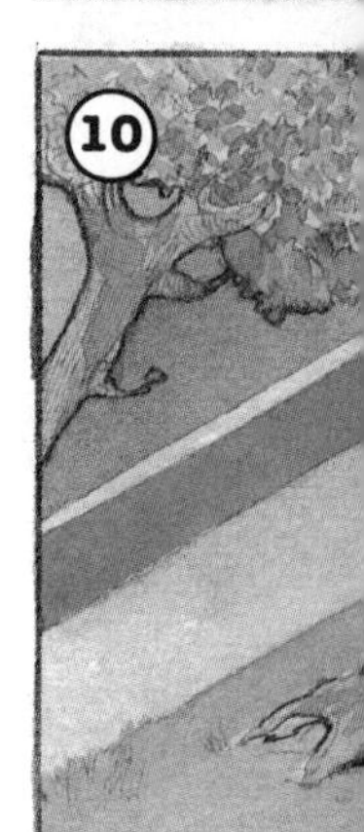

1
2
3
5
6
7
9
11
12

FOOD FOR THOUGHT

Americans eat an average of 10 pounds of chocolate each year.

According to a recent study, the average American opens the refrigerator to get food about 22 times a day.

Each year Americans eat about 700 million pounds of peanut butter—511 million pounds of it in sandwiches!

On the average, each person in the U.S. eats about 40 teaspoons of sugars and sweeteners every day. That includes sugars hidden in foods.

The first "catsup" was made in 300 B.C. in Italy. A combination of vinegar, oil, pepper, and a paste of tiny fish called anchovies, it contained no tomatoes!
There are more than 7,000 varieties of apples; how many does your supermarket carry?
Vanilla is America's favorite ice cream flavor, followed by chocolate, nutty flavors like butter pecan, chocolate chip, and strawberry.
VANILLA
About half of the salt used in the United States doesn't end up in food. It's spread on winter roads to melt ice.

THE DISAPPEARING BUBBLE

Did you know that you can hold something right before your eyes—and not see it? Even if you have perfect vision, there is always one spot where you will see nothing. It's called your blind spot, and here's a way you can find it.

Close your left eye. Hold this page at arm's length. Make sure that the boy is directly in front of your right eye. Stare at the picture of the boy.

Keep your eye on the boy. Now slowly move the page closer to you, and closer, and closer . . . until the bubble vanishes. When you can't see the bubble, you've found your blind spot.

Seeing begins when light enters your eye. The image of what you look at focuses on nerve endings at the back of your eye. These nerve endings connect with the optic nerve. The optic nerve sends a signal to your brain. At the one place where the optic nerve enters the eye, there are no nerve endings. If light is focused in that exact spot, you cannot see anything. This is your blind spot.

STUMPER

Repeat the experiment with both eyes open. Can you think of a reason why you can't find your blind spot when both eyes are open?

WATER DROP MAZE

Can you make a drop of water move through this maze?

Take a smooth piece of wax paper and cover the maze. With a sharp pencil, trace the maze path onto the wax paper.

Now, place a single drop of water at the start of the maze you have traced. You may want to use a medicine dropper to do this.

By tilting the wax paper back and forth, see if you can make the drop move through your maze. Good luck.

ANIMAL PREDICTORS

People have always tried to predict the weather. Long ago they did this by observing nature. They learned that winter comes after the leaves fall, and that a storm has passed when a rainbow appears.

Some people believe that animals sense changes in the weather. By observing the way animals act, you can make predictions. Watch the animals where you live and decide for yourself if any of them make good weather forecasters.

Here are some signs that are supposed to mean rain is on the way.

Do you believe them?

Frogs croak louder and longer than usual.

Dogs whine or act nervous, and cats get frisky as kittens.

Roosters crow later in the day.

Birds fly lower to the ground and gather on tree branches and telephone wires.

Pigs squeal more and gather sticks to make a nest.

Cows sit down in the fields and swat at bugs with their tails.

Bees and butterflies seem to disappear from the flower beds they usually visit.

Red and black ants build up the mounds around their ant holes.

Fish jump out of the water to nip at low-flying insects.

BRIGHT IDEAS

It takes light about eight minutes to travel from the sun to the earth.

The largest shadow you'll ever see is the shadow of the earth. During a lunar eclipse, the earth's shadow is seen as it moves across the moon.

Some animals make their own light. The brightest light is produced by the flashlight fish. Its light can be seen 100 feet away underwater.

The lamp in a lighthouse is surrounded by a huge lens which magnifies its light. The beam from a powerful lighthouse may be seen more than 20 miles away.

The first flashlight was built in 1898. Every part, including the battery and bulb, was made by hand.

Light travels at 186,000 miles per second. If a plane could travel at that speed it would circle the earth more than seven times a second.

The tallest candle ever built was 89 feet 1 inch high.

The first mirrors were not glass. They were polished metals like brass, silver, and gold. The first glass mirrors were made in Venice in the 16th century.

The light from a full moon is about as bright as a candle burning five feet away from you.

WEATHER WONDERS

Hailstones are usually no more than ½ inch in diameter, but sometimes they can be a lot larger. The largest hailstone on record measured 17½ inches around and weighed almost 1¾ pounds.

The strongest wind gust ever measured roared off of Mount Washington in New Hampshire at 231 miles per hour.

A thunderstorm can release 125 million gallons of water.

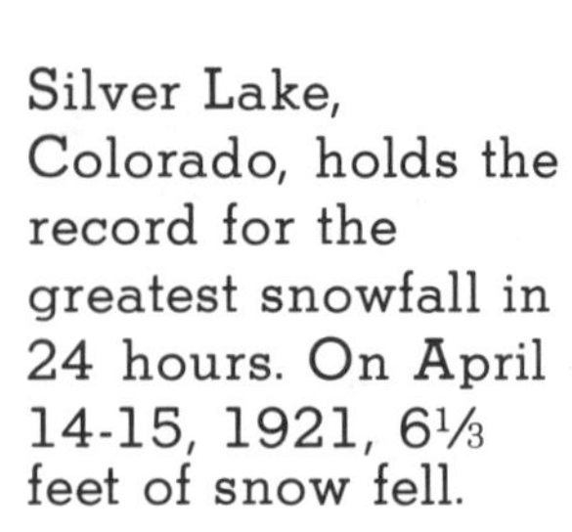

Silver Lake, Colorado, holds the record for the greatest snowfall in 24 hours. On April 14-15, 1921, 6⅓ feet of snow fell.

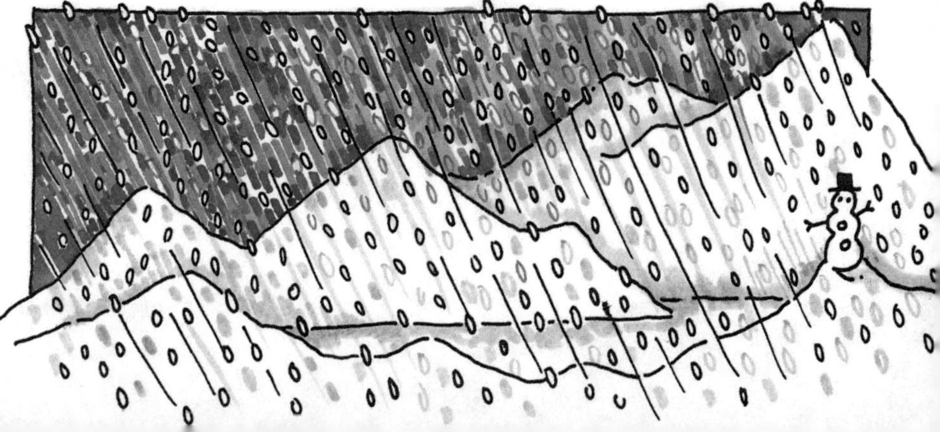

The tornado center of the world is the United States. Over 640 twisters strike our country each year.

The lowest temperature ever recorded on earth was -128.6°F at the Soviet Union's Antarctic research station.

The highest temperature ever recorded on earth was 134°F at Azizia in the Sahara Desert.

Lightning strikes the earth about 100 times each second.

Hawaii's Mount Waialeale is the rainiest place in the United States. It has rain 350 days each year.

FOOD FUN

Here is one time when it is all right to play with your food. Set up each of these food puzzles. After you solve them, you can eat the results! (Turn the book upside down to read each answer.)

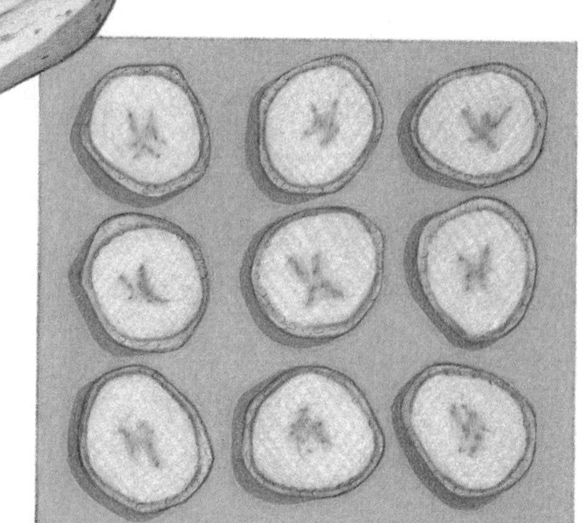

1. Slice a banana into nine pieces and lay them in three rows of three slices. Now rearrange them to make three rows of four slices.

Answer: Arrange them in a triangle with four pieces making up each side.

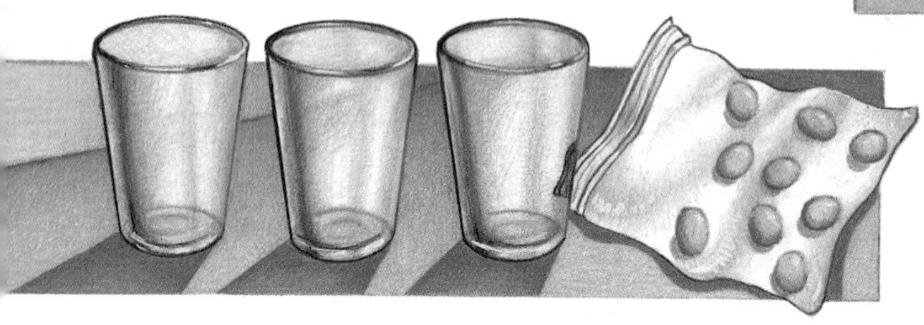

2. Place three empty cups on a table and nine grapes in a plastic bag. Can you place three grapes in each cup *and* still have three in the bag.

Answer: Take three grapes from the bag and put them in the first cup. Take three more and put them in the second cup. Now drop the bag holding the last three grapes into the third cup.

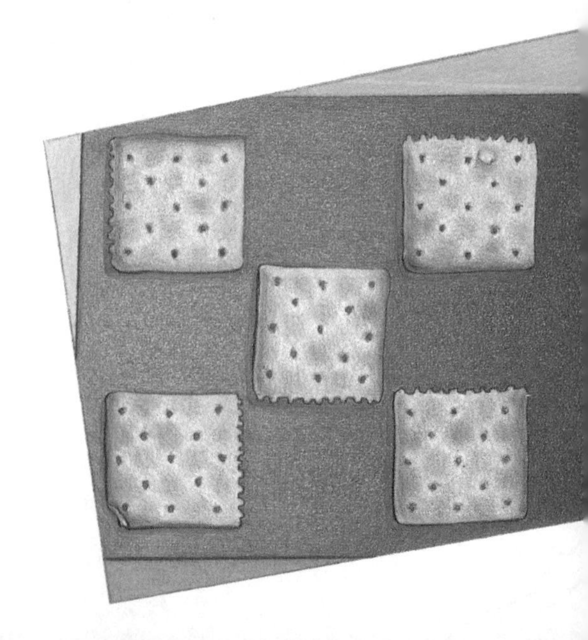

3. Place five crackers as you see here. Now add one more so that each diagonal row has four.

Answer: Place the cracker on top of the cracker in the middle.

4. Set up six cups—three empty and three containing juice—as you see in the picture. Can you arrange them so that every other cup is empty? You can move only one cup.

Answer: Pour the juice from the fourth cup into the first cup.

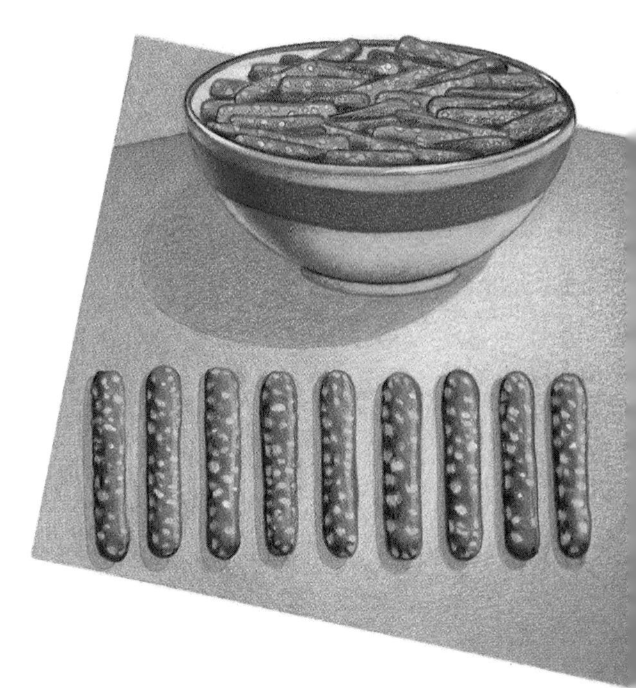

5. Set up nine pretzel sticks in a row. Rearrange them to make ten without breaking any pretzels.

Answer: Have the pretzels spell the word TEN in block letters.

6. Set up nine pretzel-stick squares as you see here. Now eat eight pretzels to leave two squares.

Answer: Leave the big square around the outside and the small square in the middle. Eat all the other pretzels.

7. Spread peanut butter on one of two crackers and place them side by side. Now pick them both up while touching only one.

Answer: Lift up one cracker. Turn it upside-down and place it on the other. Push so that the peanut butter holds the two crackers together. Now lift both without ever touching the bottom one.

WATER WOWS

When the average person takes a bath, he or she uses about 35 gallons of water.

Over six feet of rain fell in a single day on the Island of Reunion in the Indian Ocean. What would happen if that much fell where you live?

A typical thundercloud holds about six trillion raindrops.

A thirsty camel can drink about 25 gallons of water in 10 minutes. How much can you drink?

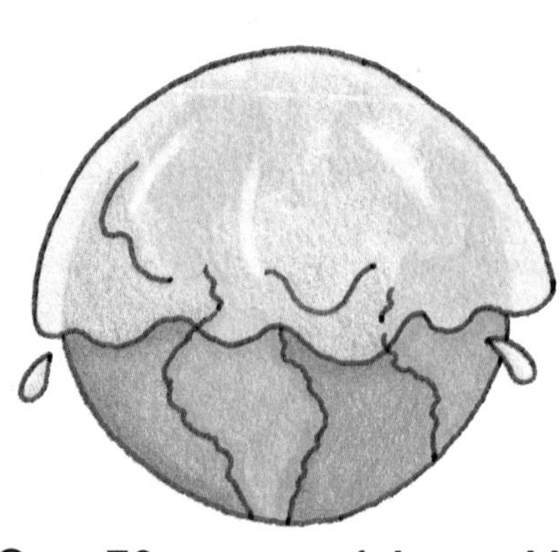

Over 70 percent of the world is covered with water.

There is enough water in the Great Lakes to cover the entire United States with 12 feet of water.

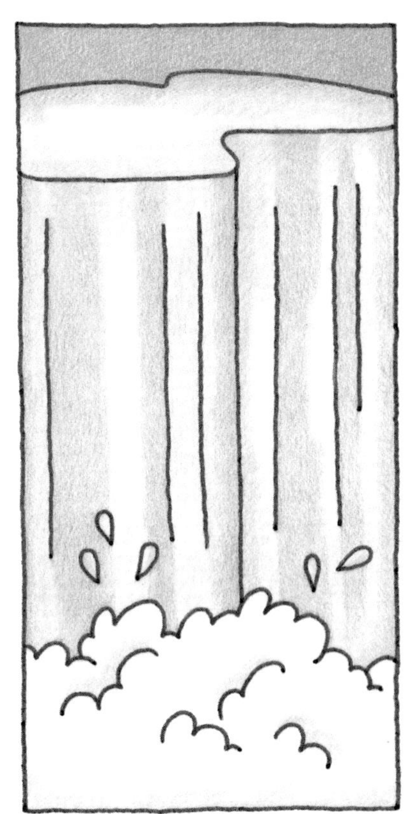

Every second, three and a half million gallons of water pour over Niagara Falls.

Your body is made up of 60 percent water.

When salt water freezes, it contains almost no salt. In some parts of the world, melted ice is used for drinking water.

HAND SHADOWS

Hand shadows are easy to make—and lots of fun. All you need are your hands, a wall, and a bright light source, like a table lamp with the shade taken off. Be careful handling the lamp and remember that the bulb can get very hot.

To make the shadows, hold your hands between the light source and the wall. The pictures here show you how to form some animals. Try experimenting a bit. Can you figure out how to make other animals? For more fun, add sound effects to your creations and put on a real show.

HOUSE OF MIRRORS

When this girl looks in the mirror, she can see a boy at the other end of the fun house. That's because light is bouncing from one mirror to the next until it reaches her eyes.

Can you follow the path of the reflecting light? Use your finger to trace the path from one mirror to the next. The dotted line will help you get started. (Remember, when light strikes a mirror at an angle, it is reflected away at the same angle.)

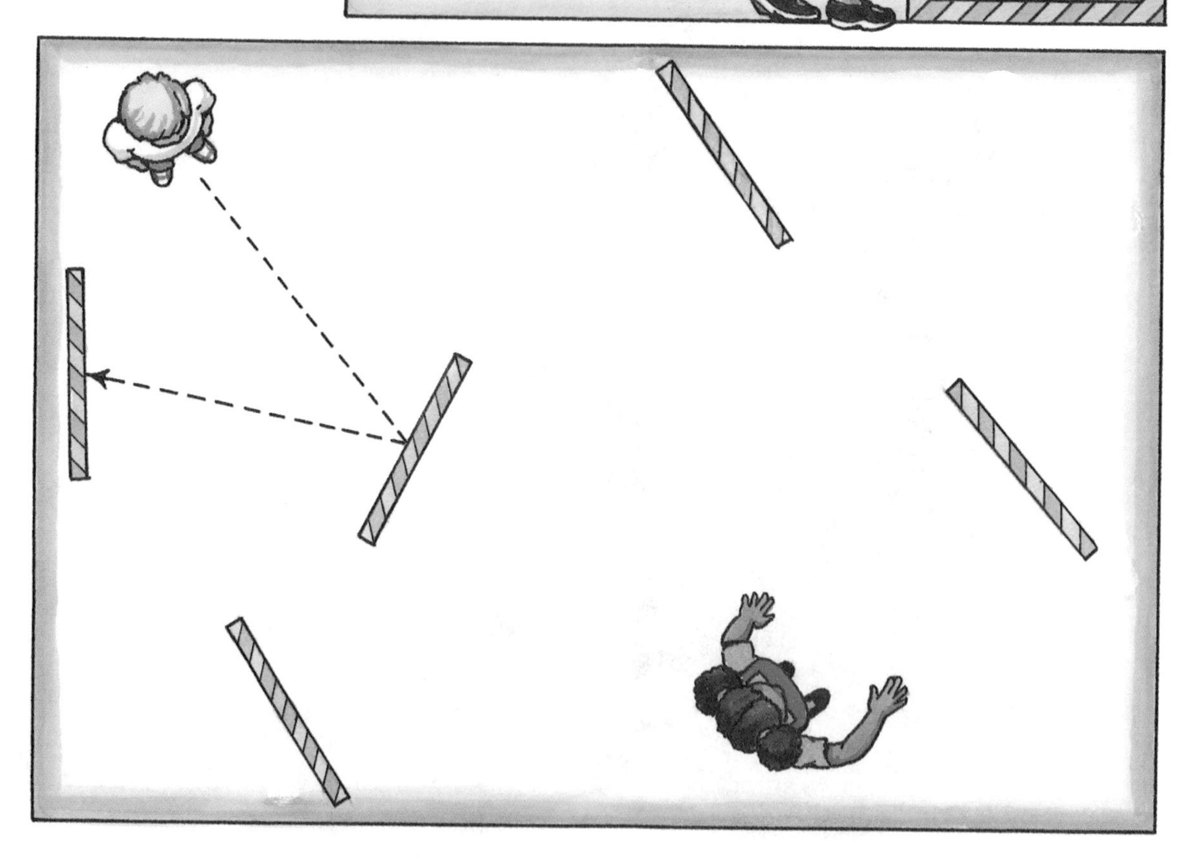

TANGLED PIPE PUZZLE

Can you predict how water will flow through this tangled set of pipes?

MAKING SENSE

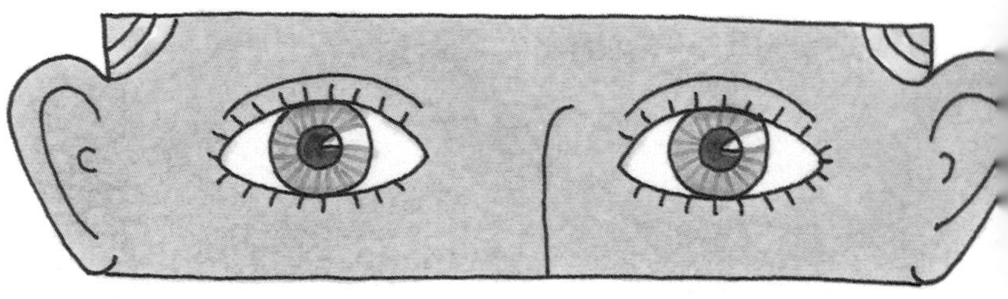

To see things clearly, your eyes must focus and refocus as many as 100,000 times a day.

Rashes and bites itch more when you are calm or trying to fall asleep because your senses are more focused on them.

Bloodhounds are famous for their sensitive noses. They have been known to pick up a scent that is five days old and follow it for fifty miles.

A cricket hears sounds through its front legs.

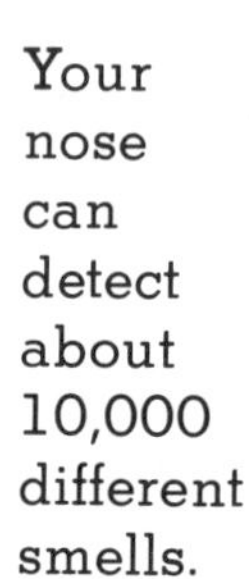

Your nose can detect about 10,000 different smells.

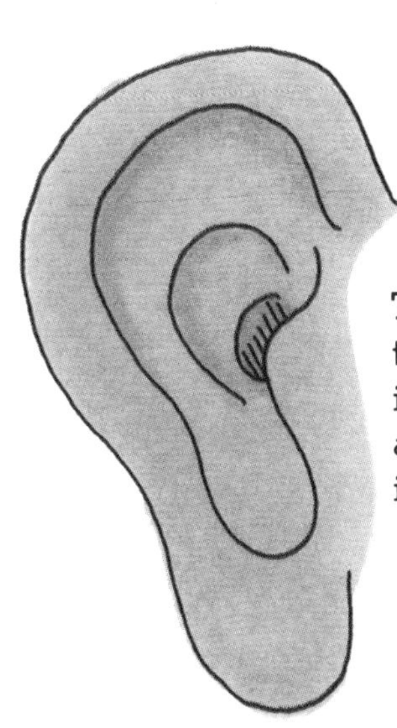

The three tiniest bones in your body are located in your ear.

Catfish have taste buds located all over the outside of their bodies.

Many animals, including rabbits, cats, rats, and sheep, love the taste of salt. Hamsters hate it.

Kids can hear higher-pitched sounds than adults can.

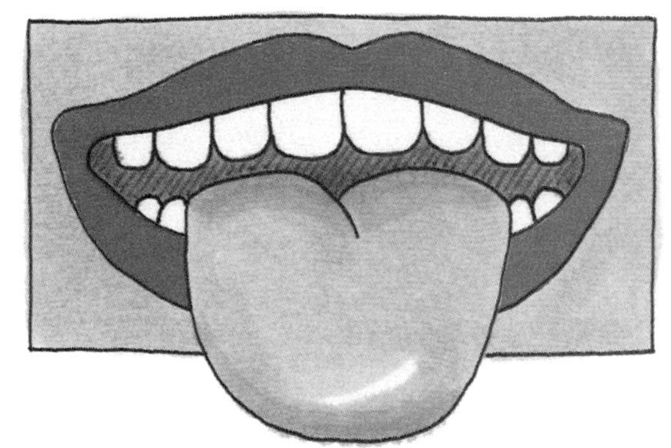

Your 10,000 taste buds are not only located on your tongue. There are buds on the inside of your cheeks and in the top part of your throat, too.

WHAT A CATCH!

If this baseball player catches that ball, his team will win the game. You can help him. Bring the book toward your face so that the tip of your nose touches the black dot. As you do this, the ball will fly into the glove.

TRY THIS

Make your own drawings that work the way this one does. Here are some you might want to try: an arrow flying through the air and striking a target; a butterfly fluttering to a flower; a rocket landing on the moon.

WAS THAT A YELLOW-PHANT?

Oscar the elephant is blue . . . but he won't be for long. Before your eyes, he will change into a yellow-phant—and your eyes will do the trick for you!

First, place this book flat on a table. Have a white piece of paper ready. Keep your head—and eyes—steady. Now, stare into Oscar's eye. Slowly count to 30. Keep right on looking at the same spot, but quickly cover Oscar with the white paper. Do you see him turn yellow? He should get bright yellow for a moment.

If you didn't see Oscar change color the first time, keep trying. Stare at him a little longer the next time.

RHYMING CALENDAR

Hundreds of years ago in England, a man named Sheridan came up with a calendar based on weather. To figure out which month is which, start in the upper left corner and read across each row. (Hint, January is Slippy.)

Super Challenge

WIND MAKER

Here's an easy way to see what causes wind. You'll just need a lamp, talcum powder, and some sheets of newspaper.

Spread out a few sheets of paper under the lamp. If the lamp has a shade, take the shade off. Turn on the lamp and wait for the light bulb to get hot. Then sprinkle a pinch of talcum powder over the light bulb and watch what happens.

When the sun heats the earth, the earth in turn heats the air nearest to the ground. The heated air rises, and cooler air moves in to take its place. This movement of the warm air and the cold air is wind. You created wind by letting the light bulb heat the air around it. The talcum powder helped you see how the air was moving.

QUICK TIP

Be careful not to touch the light bulb while you're doing this activity—it may be hot enough to burn you.

THE HOPPING COIN

You can make a plastic coin hop onto a plate without touching it. All you need is a plastic coin, like a game token, and a plate. Place the coin at the edge of a table. Push it in about a half an inch. Put the plate on the table, about six inches behind the coin. Press your chin against the table. Start blowing hard across the top of the token. Soon the coin will sail into the plate.

You've just demonstrated how strong the force of wind can be. When you blow across the top of the coin, that fast-moving wind lowers the air pressure over the coin. The pressure under the coin is now pushing up with greater force. This change in the balance of forces lifts the coin into the air and makes it sail onto the plate. This is why things like garbage pail covers and signs that aren't held down can fly through the air on a windy day—and become dangerous for anyone in their way.

QUICK TIP

If it doesn't work at first, adjust the positions of the coin and plate. If you don't have a game token handy, you can use a button instead, but a metal coin is too heavy.

SHADOW PEOPLE

Can you recognize a person from the shape of a shadow? Find out by making a shadow portrait or silhouette. All you need is a friend, a chair, a lamp without a shade, tape, a large sheet of white paper, and a pencil or marker.

Place the chair about a foot and a half away from a bare wall. Turn the chair sideways and ask your friend to sit down.

Set up the lamp so that it's about eight feet from the wall and the same height as your friend's head. Make the room as dark as possible. Turn off all of the other lights and close any shades or blinds. You should be able to see a shadow of the side of your friend's face on the wall.

Make the shadow as sharp as possible by moving the lamp closer or farther away from the wall. When the shadow is sharp, tape the piece of paper to the wall where the shadow appears.

Tell your friend to sit very still—any false move might give him two noses. Talk to your friend while you trace along the edge of the shadow—but don't make him laugh!

After you are done tracing, turn on the lights and show off your silhouette portrait. You can cut out the drawing or color it. (By the way, if you give your friend a green face, don't expect him to love it.)

OIL AND ICE

Oil and water don't mix. Put them together, and the oil will stay on top. But what happens if you mix oil and ice? Since both oil and ice float on water, which one will stay on top? And what happens when the ice starts to melt?

Make an ice cube with water and food coloring. Pick a nice rich color like blue or red. Fill a small glass a little more than half full with cooking oil. Drop the ice cube in, and watch what happens—especially when the ice begins to melt.

EYE DROPPERS

Can you see as well with one eye as you can with two? To find out, play this game with a friend.

Place a cup on a table. Stand about five feet away. Have your friend hold a penny about one foot above the table. Now, cover one of your eyes. Tell your friend how to move his hand so that when the penny is dropped it will fall into the cup. When you think your friend's hand is directly over the cup, have him drop the penny, and see what happens.

You can see clearly with one eye, but you need two eyes to judge distance. Your eyes are set slightly apart. Each one sends a picture to your brain. By blending the pictures, your brain helps you tell how far away something is.

When you cover one eye, you are less able to see things in relation to one another. This makes it harder to judge the distances between things.

It is possible to see distances with one eye. Have your friend drop pennies for you a few more times. As your brain adjusts to the situation, your ability to judge distance with one eye may get better.

RED CELERY

You've seen people eat celery, but have you ever seen celery eat? All it takes is water, food coloring, and a stalk of celery with leaves.

Mix some food coloring into a jar of water. Chop off the bottom of a stalk of celery. Stand the stalk in the jar. After a few hours, take the celery out of the water. Look at the bottom of the stalk. Those tiny spots of color are the ends of celery veins that have absorbed the water.

Put the celery back into the jar and check it in a day or two. You'll see that the leaves have begun to change color.

Plants need water to live. They draw this water upward through their veins. The water has minerals that plants use in making their own food.

STUMPER

Split a piece of celery halfway up the stalk. Put one tip in a glass with red food coloring. Put the other tip in a glass with blue food coloring. What do you think will happen?

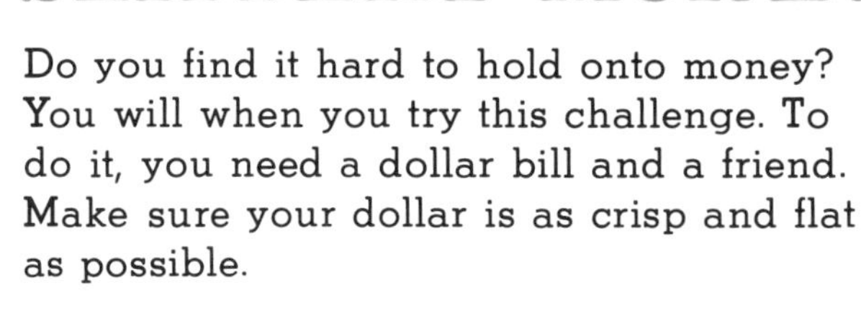

SLIPPERY MONEY

Do you find it hard to hold onto money? You will when you try this challenge. To do it, you need a dollar bill and a friend. Make sure your dollar is as crisp and flat as possible.

Have your friend hold the dollar at the top, as shown in the picture. Put your thumb and forefinger around the middle of the bill, so you will be ready to grab it. Your friend will suddenly let the dollar drop—without telling you. Can you snap your fingers shut in time to catch the bill?

Chances are the dollar will slip through your fingers before you can catch it. When you see your friend let go, your eyes send a message to your brain. A second message is sent from your brain to your hand telling you to catch the dollar. All this happens in an instant, but that's all it takes for the dollar to slip by you. The time between when your eyes see something and your body responds and moves is called "reaction time."

TRY THIS

Here is a way to measure your reaction time in inches. Repeat this challenge using a yardstick instead of a dollar. Hold your fingers at the very bottom of the yardstick. How many inches go by before you can catch the stick?

"X" MARKS THE SPOT

It's easy to touch an "X" on a piece of paper with the tip of your pencil. But what happens if you put the paper behind a jar of water?

To find out, fill a jar with water. Now draw an "X" on a piece of paper and place the paper behind the jar. Looking through the jar, try to touch the center of the "X" with your pencil tip. It's not as easy as you thought, is it?

The trick is not impossible to do. But it might take a couple of tries to get the hang of it. You will find out that where you think you are placing your pencil point and where it ends up are not the same.

Why is the "X" not where you expect it to be? The water bends the light rays coming from the "X" before they reach your eye. So the "X" is not really where you think it is.

TRY THIS

Draw a circle on a piece of paper instead of an "X". Put it behind the jar. Now try to draw in a set of eyes, a nose and a mouth while looking through the jar. How well did you do?

WATER SEESAW

You can build a simple seesaw out of a round pencil, a ruler, and two glasses of water. When you finish, you can make it move up and down in a very surprising way.

Place the pencil on the table. Tape it down so it will not move. Balance the ruler on the pencil. Make sure that neither side of the ruler is touching the table.

Add water to one of the glasses until it is about three quarters full. Put this glass on one end of the ruler.

Place the empty glass on the other end. Fill it until the two glasses of water are perfectly balanced on your seesaw.

Will the seesaw stay balanced if you dip your finger in one of the glasses? Try it and see what happens.

It doesn't seem possible, but your finger can push down the seesaw by just touching the water. When you put your finger in the glass, it takes the place of some water. The water has nowhere to go but up. The water level rises in the glass. The combined weight of the water and your finger causes the seesaw to fall. When you take your finger out of the glass, the seesaw balances.

QUICK TIP

The hardest part of this challenge is getting the seesaw to balance in the first place. If you can't do it, don't worry. This trick also works if the glasses are slightly out of balance. In that case, dip your finger in the glass on the side of the seesaw that is up and it should drift down.

RIGHT EYED OR LEFT?

You know that you are either right-handed or left-handed. But did you know that you are right-eyed or left-eyed too? Here's how to find out which one you are.

Make a circle with your thumb and forefinger. Hold the circle just above the tip of your nose. With both eyes open, look through the circle until some object nearby—a book, a lamp, a picture on the wall—falls just in the center of the circle.

Now close one eye, then the other. Watch what happens to the image in the circle. Through one eye, the book, picture, or lamp will appear to be at the side of the circle. Through the other eye, the object will remain in the center, just as it was when both eyes were open.

You are right-eyed if the image you see with just that eye open matches what you see when both eyes are open. You are left-eyed—which is much rarer—if your left eye sees the image in the middle of the circle.

SODA POP PUZZLER

Drinking soda through a straw is easy, right? If you think so, try this. Take a bottle of soda or juice and two straws. Put the ends of both straws in your mouth. Slip the other end of one straw into the soda bottle and leave the other straw outside. Now start drinking.

When you place a straw in a bottle and drink, you first suck air out of your mouth and the straw. Air pressure then pushes liquid into your mouth. When you place one straw outside the bottle, it keeps forcing air into your mouth. You can't reduce the air pressure in the soda straw. Without a change in air pressure, the soda will not be forced up the straw.

There is a way to drink the soda. You must keep the air from coming up through the outside straw. Try blocking that straw with your tongue while drinking from the other.

TRY THIS

Hold a soda pop race with your friends. Have everyone put one straw in the bottle and one straw out. How long does it take your friends to figure out that they have to block the opening of the outside straw in order to drink?

EAR SNAPPERS

You need two eyes to judge the exact distance of things you see. Do you think your two ears work together in a similar way? Grab a friend and find out!

Have your friend stand still with her eyes closed. Tell her you are going to snap your fingers. Her job will be to point as fast as possible to the sound of the snap.

Silently move to one side and snap your fingers. Keep your hand about two feet from your friend's head. After snapping several times from different spots around her, snap your fingers directly behind her and see what happens. Try a snap two feet in front of your friend's nose. What happens then?

Your two ears work together to help you find where sounds come from. A noise coming from the right reaches your right ear first. It also sounds a bit louder in that ear. Your brain compares that stronger message with the one coming from your left ear. As a result, you know where the sound is.

When a noise is directly behind you, it sounds the same in both ears. The same is true when it is directly in front of you. That's why, when your friend's eyes are closed, she may find it hard to tell front from back.

QUICK TIP

It may be hard to fool your friend even with her eyes closed. She might hear your footsteps and know where you are. Be sure to pick a spot where you can move around your friend as quietly as possible.

LIGHT SHOWER

You know that water flows and light shines.
Here's a way to make light flow and water shine.

Find an empty cardboard juice can, a large flashlight, and a sharp pencil. Use the pencil carefully to poke a hole in the side of the can near the bottom. Don't make the hole too big.

Bring the can and the flashlight into a room with a sink. While you cover the hole in the juice can with one finger, fill the can with water from the faucet. Turn on the flashlight and then turn off the light in the room. Place the flashlight over the top of the juice can so that all of the light is shining into the can. The flashlight should cover the entire open end of the can. Hold the can over the sink.

Now remove your finger that's blocking the hole, and tilt the can so water flows into the sink. The water shines, and light appears to be flowing along with the water! Jiggle the can, and watch what happens.

QUICK TIP

If light is escaping out of the sides of your flashlight, wrap the flashlight's rim with black paper. This will direct more light into the can, and into the stream of water.

EMPTY ISN'T EMPTY

Air is everywhere around you, even in an empty glass. You can prove this easily. Take a glass that seems to have nothing in it. Turn it upside down and shake it a few times to make sure.

Crumple up a paper towel and push it into the bottom of the glass so it will stay in there when you tip the glass upside down. Fill a sink with water. Holding the glass by the bottom, push it straight under the water. Keep it under the water for a few moments and then lift it out.

Check the paper. It should still be dry. If the glass were truly empty, the water would have soaked the paper. A pocket of air trapped inside the glass kept the water from wetting the paper—even after you held the glass underwater.

POURING AIR UNDERWATER

Some things sound impossible, but if you know the secret, they can be easy. Take pouring air underwater, for example. Sound impossible? Here's a way to do it. You'll need two drinking glasses and some water.

The girl in the picture is using an aquarium full of water. You can try this trick in your kitchen sink—it's easier to set up.

Put one glass in the sink and let it fill with water. When the glass is full, hold it by the bottom and pull it up. Don't take it all the way out of the water. Stop when the rim is just under the surface. The glass should be upside down but filled with water.

Hold a second glass by the bottom and push it straight down into the water. If you do this carefully, air will be trapped in the second glass. Make sure the glass of air is almost directly under the first glass. Now, tip the second glass slowly upward toward the first. Air from the second glass will bubble up into the first glass and push out water.

TRY THIS

See how many tries it takes to fill up the first glass completely with air from the second glass.

FEET FEELERS

A bath towel . . . a balloon . . . a baseball. You could probably tell them apart with your eyes closed, using your hands. But what if you felt them with your feet? Could you then tell them apart? Get together with a friend and test how well your feet "feel."

Gather some things from around your house—a wet sponge, a towel, an inflated balloon, sandpaper, a spoon, plastic wrap, a paintbrush. Ask your friend to take off his shoes and socks. Put a blindfold on your friend. Let him touch the objects with bare feet. Ask him to describe how each object feels and to try to name it. Keep score to see how many objects your friend names correctly. Then let your friend try this on you. Take off your shoes and socks and do some guessing. See who gets the best score.

Normally you feel and touch things with your hands. That's why your hands are more sensitive than any other part of your body. Your feet are much less sensitive than your hands. That's why it's harder to identify things if you can feel them only with your feet.

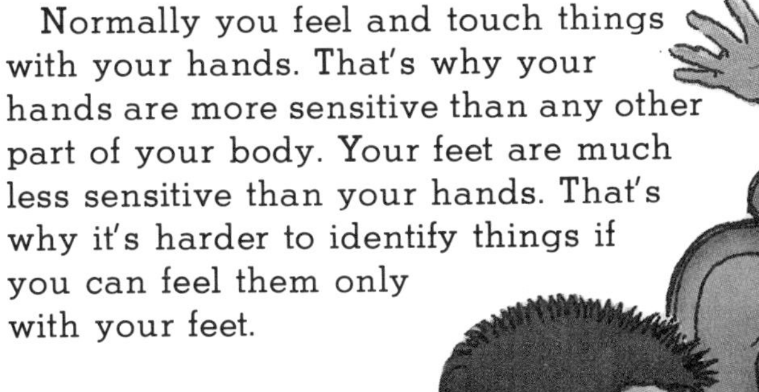

WET POTATO

How can you find out whether a potato contains water? Not by squeezing one. There's a better way. All you need is salt, a spoon, and a large raw potato.

Place the potato on a table and use the spoon to scoop out a pit. (The pit should not go all the way through the potato.) Now fill the spoon with salt and pour the salt into the pit.

Place the potato in a safe place, and wait several hours or overnight. Then look at it again. The hole you made is filled with water.

How did it get there? The salt did all the work. It drew water from the potato's cells. Salt pulls water out of people's cells, too. That's why eating salty foods makes you thirsty.

HOW MANY PENNIES?

Is a full glass of water really full? Try this and see for yourself.

Fill a drinking glass to the top with water. You may want to use a pitcher so that you can slowly pour in the water as it nears the top. Stop when you think no more water will fit. You must stop before any water spills.

Now guess how many pennies you can put in your full glass of water without making it spill over.

Take a penny and hold it just over the center of the glass. The penny should almost touch the water. Carefully drop it into the glass. Keep dropping pennies one at a time in the same way. How many did you fit before the water spilled?

We can't say how many pennies will fit, but there's a good chance that there will be more than you expect. As you add pennies to the glass, the water level rises. It actually rises above the top of the glass.

Surface tension holds the water molecules together. Eventually the water rises so high that surface tension can no longer hold it and the water spills out.

MIRROR DARTS

You can play darts at light-speed—if the darts are rays of light! You and your friends can hit a target with light rays again and again, using only mirrors.

You need two friends, two mirrors, a small flashlight, a piece of paper, a pencil or pen, tape, and a dark room.

First draw a target on the piece of paper and tape it to a wall. Give each of your friends a mirror, turn out the lights, and turn on the flashlight.

Shine the flashlight at the first mirror and watch the light bounce off. Ask your friend with the other mirror to stand in the path of the reflecting light ray. She can use the mirror to bounce the light beam toward the target. If the beam misses, shift your positions and change the way you hold the mirrors. Practice until you hit the target. Then change to new positions and try again.

Find another friend and another mirror and see if a four-person team can strike the target.

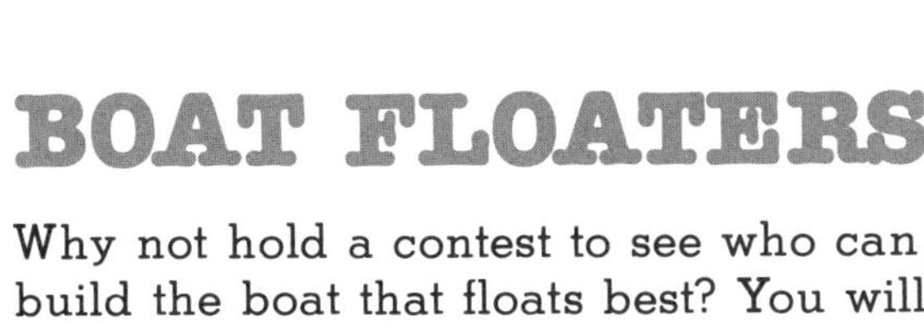

BOAT FLOATERS

Why not hold a contest to see who can build the boat that floats best? You will need some aluminum foil, lots of paper clips, and some friends. (If you don't have enough paper clips, use pennies instead.) Cut up some squares of aluminum foil that measure six inches on each side. Give one square to each of your friends. Have everyone shape the pieces of foil into boats. Fill a sink or pool with water and make sure the boats float.

Now comes the contest. Add paper clips one at a time to your boat. As the clips pile up, the boats will start sinking. Which boat held the largest cargo?

To build a better boat, you need to understand why things float. If you toss a rock into a pond, it sinks. A rock is heavier than water with the same volume. The rock's weight pulls it down and water pressure pushes it up, but the weight is greater and so the rock sinks.

Real boats weigh more than rocks, but they float because their weight is spread out over a large area. If the weight of the water pushed out of the way by the boat is more than the weight of the boat, the boat will float. So make the boat into a shape that will push the most water out of the way.

FUN WITH YOUR NOSE

How good is your sense of smell? Here are three ways to put your nose to the test. To do this, you will need the help of some friends.

SEEING SMELLS

For this first challenge, you need some inexpensive perfume and an ordinary handkerchief. Stand in the middle of a room. Close the door, and make sure no fans or air conditioners are running. Tell your friends to stand at various distances from you.

Now have everyone close his or her eyes. Without saying anything, open the perfume. Pour some on the handkerchief and hold it in the air. Have each person clap when he or she smells the perfume. From the way people clap, you can see how the odor travels through the air to fill the room.

Perfume is a liquid, but it must evaporate before you can smell it. When you hold up your wet handkerchief, some perfume enters the air. You smell it right away, but the odor must spread out and fill the room before your friends smell it too.

THE NOSE KNOWS?

Here's a nasal illusion—a trick that fools your nose.

Have a friend close his eyes. Hold a bottle of perfume just under his nose and tell him to breathe in deeply through the nose. Wait two or three minutes and then move the bottle away. Can your friend tell when the perfume is no longer there?

When an odor enters your nose, it reaches the sensitive endings of the olfactory nerve. The nerve sends a signal to your brain, which determines what your nose is smelling. At first the smell is strong, but the nerve endings gradually get tired out, and you lose your sensitivity to the smell. You don't even know when the source of the smell has been removed.

This seems odd, but your nose does this all the time. When you enter a kitchen where someone is cooking, you smell odors immediately. After a while, you no longer notice them.

THE TASTE TEST

Your senses of taste and smell work together all the time. Cut up small bits of an onion, an apple, and a potato.

Blindfold a friend and have him hold his nose. Now give him bits of food to taste. Can he tell an onion from an apple?

When you are eating, the odors of food reach your nose. That smell helps you figure out what food you are eating. When you cannot smell certain foods, it can be more difficult to tell them apart. That's also why, when you have a cold, food does not taste as good. Your stuffy nose keeps you from smelling the food you are eating.

LIGHT, SHADOW, ACTION

On a sunny morning, ask a friend to trace your shadow on the sidewalk with a piece of chalk. Then do the same for your friend. Put your initials inside so you'll remember whose shadows they are.

In the middle of the day, around noon, return to the chalk outlines and see what's happened to your shadows.

Go back to the same spots later in the afternoon. You'll find your shadows have changed once again—in a different way.

What's going on here?

The size or length of a shadow depends on whether light is hitting an object head on, or sideways at an angle.

In the morning, when the sun is rising, its rays are shining at you at an angle, so your shadow is longer. But at noon, the sun is highest, so your shadow will be shortest. Later in the day as the sun is on its way to setting, the rays are coming toward you at an angle once again—but this time from the opposite direction. So your shadow is long again, but now it stretches away from the chalk outline.

TRY THIS

Shadow Tag is a fast-moving game. In order to catch another player, whoever is "it" has to step on someone else's shadow and shout out his or her name. One good strategy to keep from being caught is to hide your shadow in the shadow of something bigger, like a nearby building. Why is this game harder to play at noon than at other times of the day?

PAPER WORMS

You can turn the paper wrapper from a straw into a squirming worm. All it takes is a drop of water. This is a good trick to try in a restaurant, since you need a straw, a glass of water, and the straw's paper wrapper.

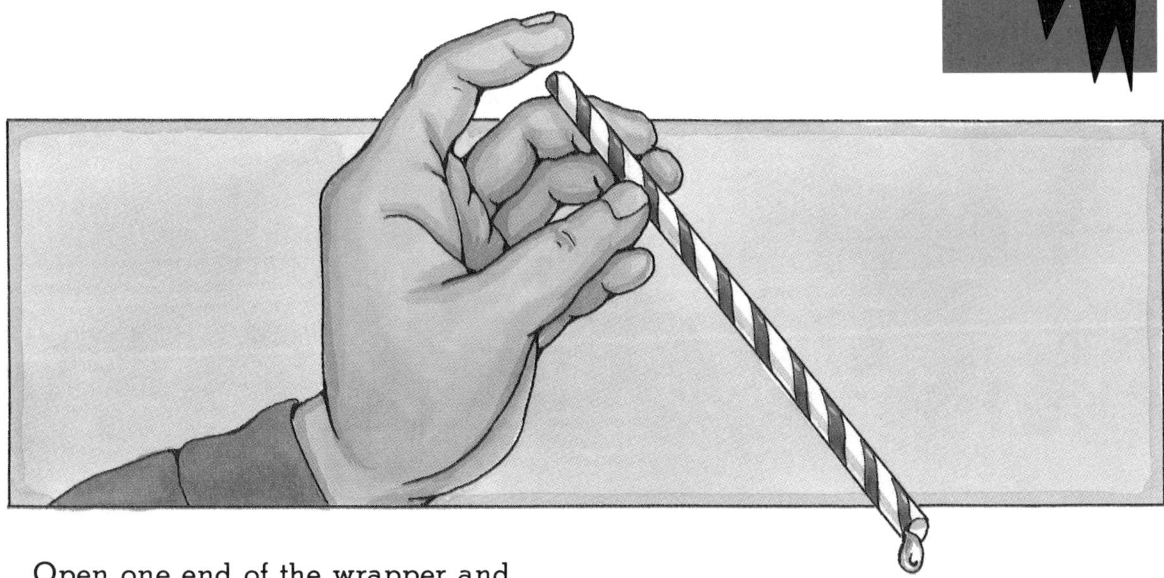

Open one end of the wrapper and pull it down so that it scrunches into a small piece of paper. Take it off the straw. Dip one end of the straw in the water. Place your finger over the other end. When you lift the straw out of the glass, the water stays in the straw. But, when you take your finger off the end, the water pours out. Practice until you can get only a single drop of water to come out.

Then, using your straw, place a drop of water on one end of the scrunched-up wrapper. Watch as the "worm" wriggles and grows before your eyes.

Your worm wriggles because of the way the water moves through the paper. Paper is made of many tiny, pressed-together fibers. The water drop on the end of the paper travels from one fiber to the other. Eventually, the whole wrapper becomes soaked. As the water moves through the paper, the wrapper straightens out. It almost seems alive as it wriggles and untwists.

SLOW MOTION SWIRLS

Have you ever mixed two colors of paint together? The swirling patterns are beautiful, but they disappear too quickly. With cornstarch, food coloring, and water, you can make the same kind of patterns that move in slow motion.

You will need a shallow container, like a baking dish or pie pan. Put about an inch of water in the pan. Slowly add six teaspoons of cornstarch and stir to get rid of any lumps. The liquid should look like skim milk.

Wait until the liquid stops moving in the pan. Then hold a bottle of blue food coloring about three inches above it. Squeeze a drop into the middle of the liquid.

Next, slowly pull the tip of a drinking straw in a straight line through the middle of the floating drop of color. (If you don't have a straw, you can use a stick or a thin spoon handle.) Watch the patterns that form as the color floats slowly in the liquid.

TRY THIS

Add drops of yellow, red, and green to the liquid. Move the straw slowly through them. What kind of patterns did you create? Try moving the straw in a slow circle.

MAZE IN A MIRROR

This maze looks simple, but try it with an added challenge. Stand a mirror along the side of the maze. Now move your finger along the correct path, while looking at the maze in the mirror.

TRY THIS

Draw a squiggly line on a piece of paper. Now make an exact copy on a piece of paper for each of your friends. (You can trace this or make a duplicate with a copy machine.) Have everyone look in a mirror and follow the squiggle with a pencil. Who finished first? Who did the neatest job?

WATER BRIDGE

Most bridges are made so people can cross over water. Can you make a bridge for water to travel across? To find out, you will need a pitcher of water, a string, and an empty bowl or glass.

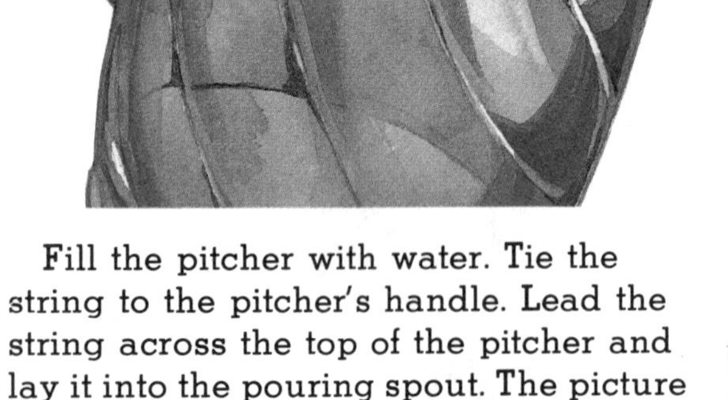

Fill the pitcher with water. Tie the string to the pitcher's handle. Lead the string across the top of the pitcher and lay it into the pouring spout. The picture shows you how to place the string.

Put the other end of the string into the empty container. Hold the string tightly against the inside. Gently pour the water so it moves across the string and into the empty container. If the water spills, pour more slowly. You may need to experiment a few times. When you get it just right, the water will cross your "bridge" and land in the bowl at the other end.

QUICK TIP

Your water bridge will work because bits of water tend to stick together and to the string. The challenge is to pour gently enough to keep the water sticking together on the string. If you pour too hard, the stream will break apart and spill.

AIR SCALE

With two balloons and a yardstick, you can make a scale to show that air has weight.

Blow up two balloons to the same size. Tape one to each end of the yardstick. Tie a string to the middle of the yardstick. Hang it from one end of a pencil (as you see in the drawing). Place the other end of the pencil under a pile of heavy books to keep it in place.

Adjust the yardstick until the balloons are balanced and the yardstick is straight. If you've blown up the balloons to the same size, they should evenly balance on the yardstick. Now pop one balloon and watch what happens.

You've let the air out of the popped balloon, but the other balloon still holds air. In fact, because you had to blow up the balloon it has extra air pressure inside. The weight of this extra air pulls the yardstick down.

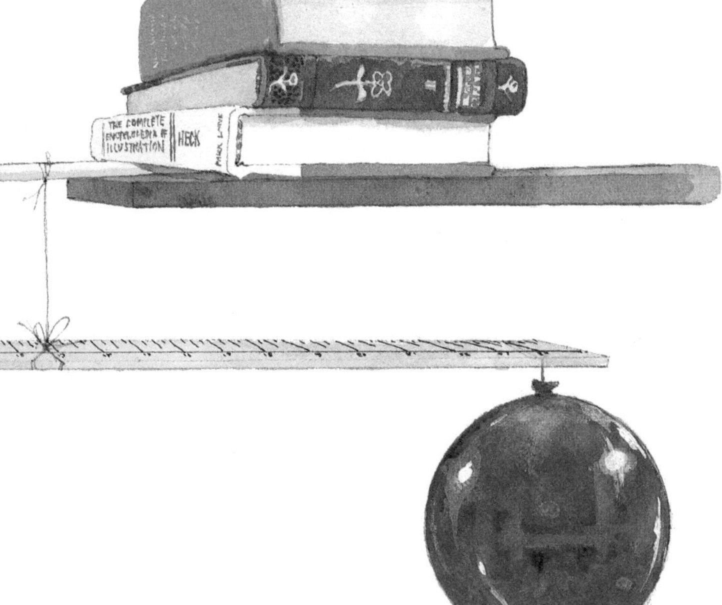

When your balloon pops, a piece of it may fall off your scale. If that happens, your balloons aren't of equal weight anymore. Try again with a new balloon.

BACKWARD REFLECTION

Usually, when you look in a mirror, left and right are reversed. Is it possible to look in a mirror without this happening?

To find out, you will need two hand mirrors. The mirrors don't have to be the same size, but they cannot have frames. You will also need something that obviously appears backward in a mirror. You could use a small clock with numbers on it. Or write your name on a piece of paper.

Place the clock on a table. Hold one mirror in front of it so you see how the clock looks. Now stand the mirrors side by side with their edges touching. Move them so the angle changes and watch what happens in the mirrors. Can you make the clock read correctly?

The secret is to have two mirrors working at just the right angle. When that happens, light bounces from the clock face, to one mirror, to the other, and finally to your eyes. The first mirror reverses the image left and right. The second mirror reverses it back again. As a result, the image that reaches your eyes is not reversed.

Index

The experiments and activities in this book can be categorized into five basic science areas of study: food, light, senses, water, and weather. This index is organized by topic alphabetically within each area of study.

FOOD

LIGHT

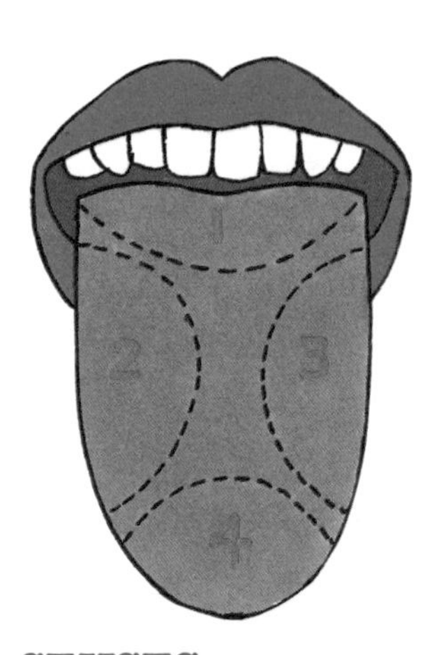

SENSES

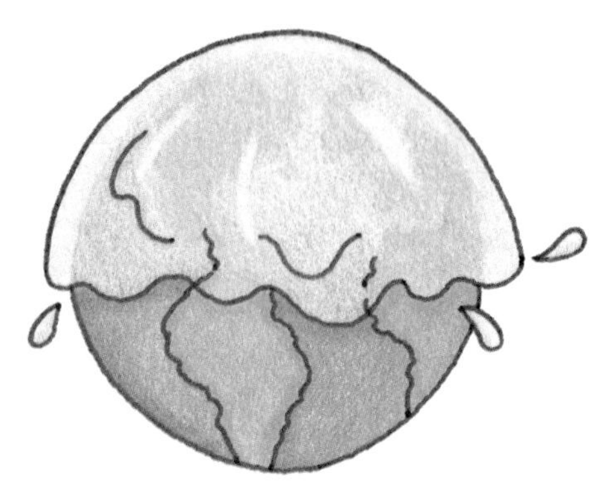

WATER

WEATHER